MISSOURI MADNESS

A Novel By

MICHAEL FREDERICK

Michael Frederick

Jan, 2001/ 1st printing

Novels by author:
"LEDGES"
"THE PAPER MAN"

This book is a work of fiction
And represents no actual persons
living or dead in any way whatsoever.

Dedicated to Brother John

Jerome

     It's March 2000. To Jack Dunn, March was the month in which many times he had just pounded things out until he had something good going that gave him hope for prosperity. Not this March, and not in the last century could he make things prosper. It was all survival, that's all it was for J. D. The cynical bumper sticker on his old car said it all: "Different day . . . Same bullshit." Yes, it was getting harder and harder to get out of bed in the morning, even on weekends. America had lied to him--do one thing well and you will prosper. Bullshit! He did do one thing better than anyone in the country: He was the best telemarketer in the friggin' world, the King of Slugs (sedentary living under great stress) and anyone who worked with him knew it.

     Last weekend, J. D. took inventory of his meager possessions in his studio apartment in Council Bluffs, across the river from Omaha. He threw things away he thought were useless in an attempt to clear his past. An old friend had told him that Faulkner claimed there is no past. Bullshit! If the past isn't real then Faulkner would have had nothing to write about. Those that believe that crap cannot handle their past; so, they deny it exists and go on pretending to be living in the moment, ignoring their histories that the subconscious reveals to them in dreams and every time they pause to think or reflect on every action they make. Bullshit!

     Those were J.D.'s thoughts today after he rolled off his floor mattress, painfully stretched his near-fifty-year-old body, plopped into his hot bath, shaved, brushed his teeth, and got dressed in the old clothes he kept new-looking by constantly caring for them. You'd never find his work clothes draped over a chair or on the floor. That was in the past, so long ago, when he lived in

1

his car drifting from telemarketing jobs from Charleston to San Diego.

Every place he worked, even if for only a day, he had made a lifelong impression, because he could never be beaten on the phone. Contest prizes, top quotas, a better way of saying things, a magic voice that couldn't be hung up on, and good looks--all were his . . . in the past. Of these, the only one he was losing was his good looks, and that was bothering him as he drove into Omaha on his way to work. Gone were the days when he'd check himself out in the rearview mirror and see a woman looking at his handsome features full of youth. But today, cologne, hair-thickening gel, his position as a manager, and his voice; something in his sound was his most appealing feature now, along with his ability to really listen. He discovered long ago that in order to be a good listener you must believe in the past and know where they were coming from. In a person's voice he could hear truth, pain, love, fear and bullshit. Millions of short conversations with strangers had trained him to listen like a baby, without ever thinking about what he was going to say next.

He wished he could turn his talent into money. For a single male who never married and was closing in on fifty, he had to have money or he was doomed to live alone and struggle till he died. Living check-to-check was making him old and turning him more cynical and fearful of play. He must've had a thousand employees and fired five times that many, and dismissed a thousand times that many when the endless ads were answered over the dozens of times he'd mustered enough money to launch another small-time venture on the phone. Not just any slug could work for him; they had to be good on the phone or they were gone within a day, or an hour, or after a few calls.

"God, I'm tired," he sighed out loud. Find me a way out of this madness.

Since hitting forty, he'd only been able to date women that worked for him--telemarketers.

"Rita," he said out loud while waiting at a red light ten minutes from his office. Then, he did look at his hair in his mirror.

Most of the women he dated were average-looking, unhappy divorcees impressed with his status as their manager. But not Rita.

As traffic zipped around his '85 Olds, his thoughts changed to the rampant hurry people are in in America, lost people in a hurry to go nowhere. The new century is seventy days old and even in Omaha thousands of minds are focussed on their trifle little time schedule that's completely man-made and loaded with fear. The same fear he could feel and hear ten feet away from his mattress every night just under the floor where a rat was gnawing away at the wood, getting closer to him, and would some night gnaw his throat while he slept and drink his blood dry, he imagined.

Since the new century, these bizarre thoughts would come and go for J. D. on his drive to work in this telemarketing capital of the world. Jack, called J. D. since five years old, always believed he'd be rich by now as he parked his car in his parking space marked "Telemaster Sales Manager."

When he got out of his car, he noticed a dime-size coffee stain on his beige slacks near his zipper. He rolled his eyes and shook his head in disgust while shining the tops of his only pair of dress shoes on the back of each calf. He knew he needed an adjustment from his chiropractor and reminded himself to call his doctor after slipping on the snow-covered sidewalk.

The elevator door opened to the third floor that Telemaster leased. His 6'1" medium frame is slouched to 5'11" as on every Wednesday when he greeted Marsha, the receptionist, while sorting through his messages.

"Hump day, Marsha. Halfway there. Everybody show?"

"Natalie in non-smoking will be a couple hours late. She had to take her baby to the doctor. All the smokers are in."

Still reading his messages, J. D. entered the smokers' boiler room where a portable radio near the coffee maker played rock music. The chain-smoking telemarketers' phone chatter picked up in volume markedly as their manager opened his office door marked "Jack Dunn, Sales Manager."

His black vertical blinds were open in his small office. He twisted them shut to diminish the intensity of the morning sun. He got seated behind his cluttered desk, loosened his tie, donned his headset and dialed a phone number from one of his messages.

"Joe, please. This is J. D. returning his call from Telemaster."

Just then, the King of Slugs pushed the play button on a cassette player on his desk and held the cassette player near his headset microphone. The tape played the sound of another telephone ringing as:

"Hi, Joe! J. D. at Telemaster! Yes! We're the company that telemarkets to businesses for restaurants who offer a 2-for-1 lunch or dinner special. Would you please hold briefly, Joe? Thanks."

J. D. pushed the mute button on his headset, turned off the cassette player, calmly lit a cigarette, then leaned back in his high-back chair and smiled up at the unframed Bahamas travel poster on the wall behind him. He gazed at the poster with the color photo of a beautiful native woman wearing a bikini while walking along the Caribbean beach. J. D. pressed his mute button on his headset.

"Thanks for holdin', Joe! Joe...our service is perfect for you!"

Later that morning, J. D. came out of his office looking haggard, rubbing his sore neck as the smokers' pitch level increased. J. D. walked over to a cubicle and took a cigarette from a telemarketer's pack while he listened to another unsuspecting telemarketer's tenuous phone pitch. The manager went over to the slug's cubicle and with his middle finger, pressed down the flash hook and said in a sarcastic whisper:

"Just wondering? Maybe? I hope? This isn't survey work. Follow the script."

The intimidated slug nodded yes. J. D. stashed his unlit cigarette in his shirt pocket before entering a door marked "Non-Smokers." A dozen non-smoking slugs, mostly women, are on their phone headsets with soft classical music playing in the background. Rita, a 30-year-old bookwormish blonde wears a conservative dress with her hair tied back. She smiled at her boss as he approached her cubicle. While Rita talked with a prospect, J. D. dropped a folded note onto her desk before exiting the room. She opened the note and read "Wanna dance?" She smiled at the note.

Later that afternoon after saying goodnight to Marsha, the receptionist, J. D. stepped inside the empty office elevator, pressed the ground floor button on the panel, stepped back against the elevator wall and exhaled deeply as the elevator door closed.

Within twenty minutes, J. D.'s lying face down on his chiropractor's treatment table. His chiropractor, Doctor White, is finding sublexations on his patient's spine and pressing vertebrae into place. The doctor popped his neck on each side at timed exhalations. Then, his hips are adjusted.

"Very good," smiled Doctor White. "J. D., are you still having that numbness in your dialing hand?"

"In the morning when I first wake up," J. D. flexed and closed his dialing hand.

"Now let's have you turn over on your back and cross your arms in front of you. That's it."

Doctor White placed a hand under his patient's upper back and released a sublexation with J. D.'s exhalation on two different adjustments.

"Very good," the doctor smiled.

The doctor stood behind his patient's head waiting for his patient's exhalation as he held J. D.'s skull, twisting it left--pop! Then to the right--pop!

"There we go," White smiled. "Do you still sleep on your side?"

"Yeah."

"Try sleeping on your back. See if that helps."

"Okay."

Later that night--Ladies Night--J. D. had changed clothes to go out as he drove his car up to a bank ATM. He inserted his bank card, dialed his code and angrily swiped his card back after the ATM informed him his account was overdrawn. He looked at his near-empty gas gauge, knuckle-punched his steering wheel, then drove away, headed for downtown Omaha's Old Town district, a square mile of old warehouses renovated into expensive gift shops, restaurants, bars and nightclubs.

He sat alone at a table in a busy club across the dance floor near the disc jockey's station, when a waitress brought J. D. a mixed drink. She's seen that look before.

"On your tab, J. D.?"

"I love you."

The waitress handed J. D. a folded note. "You have an admirer."

He followed the eyes of the waitress to the bar. The waitress left. It's Rita, the non-smoking telemarketer he gave the note to. She looked stunning seated on a barstool wearing a provocative black dress with visible cleavage; her long legs crossed and facing him as she waved at her manager, her black heels pointing down as if excited. He waved back, then opened the note that read "Yes!". He smiled at the note, then made eye contact with the DJ at his control booth. The man nodded at the King of Slugs.

Before long, Anita Baker's 'Caught Up In the Rapture' began to play. He could see Rita turn down vulture after vulture. Every eye in the club watched the sexy blonde seductively walk toward J. D.'s table. He saw her coming through the maze of parting gawkers, but he turned away as if he did not know she was coming his way. He could feel and see the room focussing on her every step. Then she stood before him, smiling down at the surprised look on his face. He pretended to be shy, looking around the room at the men and their envious stupefaction. She laughed at the game he was playing to the room as he took a big drink from his whiskey and water and held her there for them to see. Then, he got up and walked to the dance floor with Rita trailing close behind. The men watched her sensually slow-dance with him in gape-jawed amazement like jackals as she laughed into his neck and grinded him slowly to the music.

"You know how many men would like to be me right now?" he whispered.

She kissed his neck and behind his ear before biting his

earlobe as they turned ever-so-slowly in a small circle.

Later that night, Rita's driving her new Jag, following close behind the '85 Olds. She squinted at his bumper sticker-- "Different day...Same bullshit" as J. D. sprayed breath freshener into his mouth.

Later in his dark studio apartment, Rita's naked, on top of J. D. on his floor mattress after making anything but love. She tried to roll off him but he pulled her down onto his chest.

"My doctor said I should sleep on my back."

Rita laughed, staying on him. She kissed his shoulder, whispering "I've got to go home. I can't miss work."

"You could get fired," he smiled, nearly asleep.

She laughed. He could hear her getting dressed in the dark. After his door closed, he shifted to his side and went to sleep with the sweet scent of her perfume all around him.

Next morning, J. D.'s walking toward his office sorting through his messages when he heard a slug make a big mistake. The phone chatter diminished as the King of Slugs pressed down the slug's flashhook.

"Nobody...in this company...asks prospects how they are today. You don't really care how they are, and they know it. It's stale, phoney, empty pretension. Their friends don't ask how they are...and you are not their friend."

"Have a real day."

The phone room chatter picked up as their manager entered his office, closing the door behind him after Marsha handed him a cup of coffee.

Seated behind his desk, he saw the message marked urgent that read "Call Albert Linn in Jerome." He dialed the number, mumbling:.

"Albert Linn...where have I heard that name?" Then he remembered---Chief Geronimo. Albert was the town cop in Jerome where Grandpa Dunn lived. He hadn't been to Jerome since he was a boy. Did Grandpa Dunn die? he wondered. He must be in his nineties.

On phone: "Albert Linn?"

The old man's voice answered yes.

"This is Jack Dunn."

J. D. sat up straight upon hearing the news that his grandfather passed away in his sleep last night and that J. D. was his sole surviving relative.

"How'd you get my number?"

He told him he got his number from a Christmas card in his grandfather's room. J. D. remembered how he always sent a Christmas card to him and put his work number on the card if he ever wanted to call him. He had put his number on maybe twenty cards and was never called. He started to feel guilty for not calling his forgotten Grandpa Dunn, then Albert told him he'd better get in touch with his grandpa's attorney in Hannibal.

"Where is he? No...my grandpa."

J. D. scribbled down Larson Funeral Home in Hannibal, told him he'd be in Jerome tomorrow and thanked him for calling. After hanging up, he remembered something. Chief Albert had let him turn on the siren in his police car when he was five or six years old. To himself--why didn't I say something to Albert? It's as if I never knew him. He scolded himself for not remembering his grandpa's best friend as he got his road atlas from a drawer and found Jerome, a tiny dot with 250 souls not too far west and a bit north of Hannibal, Missouri. He scanned the best route to get there: 80-East halfway across Iowa to 63, drop south on 63 all the way to Kirksville, maybe 40 miles south of the Iowa border. Get a motel in Kirksville, then 20 miles south on 63 to Ashland, then west some 12 miles on an unmarked county road to Jerome.

"It's in the middle of nowhere," he mumbled upon seeing that in order to get to Hannibal from Jerome he would have to drive another unmarked county road south to 36, then east some 40 miles to Hannibal.

He thought about the old man who had been his only living relative, and the fact his Grandpa Dunn was loaded. He raked his tired eyes over his cluttered desk, then around his office--the office of a man with no roots or future...until now. Only his Bahamas poster was worth taking with him. He took down the poster and rolled it into a cylinder while exiting his office. He decided to go back and get his telephone headset, disconnecting it from his phone, putting the battery compartment holder in his back pocket and placing the headset around his neck. J. D. left his office, hopefully for the last time.

The King of Slugs walked in a daze past the phone chatter into the owner's office. Marsha tried to stop him.

"J. D.! He's with a client!"

J. D.'s boss was surprised to see his manager come into his office when he's with a big client. J. D. sat down on a chair near the desk, oblivious to their meeting.

"Something wrong, J. D.?"

He didn't answer his boss. His boss excused himself and ushered his client out of his office, soon returning to sit near J. D.

"My grandfather died. I've gotta go there...to Missouri. I'm the executor of his estate."

The owner of Telemaster didn't want to lose J. D.

"Jack, I'm sorry..."

"Can I get paid up-to-date?"

The boss removed his checkbook from his desk drawer. While writing out his check:

"You need an advance?"

"No, thanks."

"Jack, you get away for a couple weeks...take care of your business...come back refreshed, huh?"

"Yeah."

J. D. stood, took his check and left the office like a zombie, with his poster in one hand, his check in the other, and his headset looped around his neck with its cord dangling to his knees.

"Take all the time you need, Jack!"

He left the building without a word to anyone. From the moment he heard about the death of his grandpa, nothing here was important to him. On his way to his apartment, he stopped at the bank and cashed his check and closed his account. For the most part, his car will be jam-packed with his shabby wardrobe and scanty belongings in a couple of hours. His last thing to handle in Omaha is to leave a note with his apartment manager explaining he had to move out right away because of a death in the family.

He cruise-controlled 65 mph on 80 East, leaving the Omaha skyline in the early afternoon with Steve Warner's song "Ain't Nothin' Like the Love of a Small Town Girl" playing on his Olds radio.

Retired Albert Linn returned from his daily mile-walk with so much on his mind he couldn't recall what the weather was like around Turtle Lake, three miles north of Jerome. The pain in his legs seemed to ache more than usual today.

I have to call him, he decided while getting the phone number from his address book. He dialed the Florida number on his black rotary phone before he could change his mind. The nurse answered the phone.

"Mr. Cochrand's residence."

"Mr. Cochrand, please."

"Who's calling?" a middle-aged woman's voice demanded coldly.

"Albert Linn in Jerome."

"I will see if he will take this call."

She dropped the phone purposely-hard onto the lace doily on the cherry wood table. She knew that any call from Jerome was bad news and affected her patient's blood pressure to life-threatening levels. Her name is Muriel Best. She moved into Mr. Cochrand's Boca Raton villa eleven years ago. She couldn't get it out of her mind ever since she heard that dreadful name--Jerome.

Mr. Cochrand's in bed, sitting up with two pillows behind his remarkable head. His eyes are closed. She knew that he knew she was there and that the phone call was for him. Robert T. Cochrand was two months shy of his 100th birthday and looked it. She'd always seen that pain in his gray eyes; she knew it came from Jerome. She had told her niece something had aged him beyond his years in his youth, and that was too bad for such a hard-working nice man as Mr. C.

She saw the fingers of his right hand twitch open to take the phone's receiver before he opened his eyes. She stood beside him holding the receiver to his wrinkled, sun-spotted ear and she listened to the call without the slightest bit of self-consciousness.

The old man whispered into the receiver.

"Yes."

"Bob..this is Albert Linn in Jerome."

"Yes," Cochrand said feebly.

"Ray Dunn passed away."

A long pause until Albert asked if he remembered Ray.

"Yes, of course I do," Cochrand snapped.

"Ray's grandson will be here tomorrow. I thought you should know.."

"Thanks for calling."

She put the receiver on the flashhook and began reading his pulse while his eyes closed again. His heart was beating faster, but not to a degree she couldn't control. She wanted to ask him about the call and yet didn't want to risk another stroke. She kept quiet after telling her patient:

"Breathe, Mr. C...breathe."

There was nobody special he had to say goodbye to in Omaha. He liked it that way. The roller coaster ride over rolling farmland on I-80 in Western Iowa in late March, with hardly any traffic, and clear road with dirty frozen slush on the shoulder, gave him a mind set to think of his life as unlived. His parents had died nine months apart in '97; he's an only child with no formal education; he's had a hundred jobs, mostly marketing things with the idea he'd get rich; never married and no kids-- at least that he knew of.

"Where had the last thirty years gone?" he asked himself out loud.

Now with Grandpa Dunn gone, he is officially alone, though he's considered himself alone, a true loner, for the last thirty years. How did it happen? he wondered. It seemed like everyone could sense I'm supposed to be alone and unknowable. A man my age is supposed to have met a good woman by now and have a good friend or two.

He looked in his rearview mirror at the eyes that were now more gray than blue. The older he got, the more gray in his eyes. His mother's eyes turned gray when she reached middle-age. Then it came back to him, as if seeing his image sparked his memory.

He thought he was seven when he first visited his Grandpa Dunn in Jerome. 1957 seemed about right. It was summertime because he was on summer vacation from his grade school in Kansas City. "Geronimo" was how he pronounced Jerome on Albert's police car. Even Ray called his best friend Geronimo some forty years later. Grandpa Dunn's first name was Raymond, the same as J. D.'s father.

He recalled Grandpa Dunn hammering steps up a tree trunk beside Grandpa's little white house, then he built a treehouse for him on a weekend during his month-long visit. He remembered handing him planks of wood and nails, and the words his grandfather said:

"This treehouse will be your special place where anything's possible."

So, he had a place to escape to whenever he visited.

He could remember the humid nights in Grandpa's treehouse, how the wind would blow through the cracks and whip open that door Grandpa made from a shower curtain, using shower curtain rings that slid over a wooden rod he cut to fit the doorway.

"Is it still there?" he wondered out loud.

Then it came back to him, something he hadn't really thought about in decades. Oz. Then out loud:

"Oz," he said slowly and deliberately.

It was after watching the Wizard of Oz on Grandpa's black and white TV he decided to name the treehouse Oz. Not just the treehouse--the entire oak tree and its 'special place' he named Oz. He never told a soul he named it Oz. But it was his special kingdom where he could sit on an old rug Grandma Dunn gave him from a rusty cabinet in the cellar.

Grandma Dunn died soon after that first summer visit. He can still see her walking with her bad hips like a penguin, bringing him his lunch in a wrinkled paper sack like the lunches she made Grandpa to carry to work. She would leave it at the base of Oz with J. D. printed on the outside. She'd always call up to him with such a serious smile.

"J. D., now you eat yer lunch and save the bag!"

He'd scramble down Oz and back up again. He'd sit on that old rug and eat her egg salad sandwiches shaped in those perfectly wedged halves; an apple, an orange, or a banana with those homemade big cookies that never failed to cover the air with the scent of good home cooking done with love. He knew Grandma Dunn had died minutes before he was told by his mother. That's why he took that job in Virginia Beach telemarketing office supplies twenty years ago, so he could be near the Edgar Cayce Institute. It was that memory of knowing Grandma died before he was told that sent him there to find out more about the Sleeping Prophet who healed and amazed so many people.

He remembered her funeral and Grandpa's face looking straight ahead at her casket from the front row in the little church. J. D. sat next to him with his parents on his right side. He thought it odd that there was no crying around him, only that stare of Grandpa's and that ramrod-straight back that looked so strong and enduring and so full of memories of his beloved mate. The day after the funeral, Grandpa looked happy. It was his faith in heaven that made his eyes shine. Why didn't my father have that faith like Grandpa? he wondered many times growing up, knowing his father and Grandpa Dunn were not close at all. How does a father not pass that kind of faith on to his son? he wondered. And what kind of life would I have now if he had, he mused. He had parents who never took him to church, except for weddings and funerals.

He lit a cigarette and noticed he'd driven forty miles, passing the Ashland exit on 80. Was Faulkner right? he thought. Is there no past? It all seemed like a dream and unreal. Back then, he could only blame it all on his mother, for she had put up with his father's money-grubbing scramble to be rich. His father failed, too.

"Like I have," he snorted, blowing out his smoke toward his open window. Most good parents would instill a sense of family during holidays, sending at least a card.

"I don't even know Grandpa's birthday," he snorted again, noticing his grip on the wheel way too tense, so he diminished it with an underhand grip at the bottom of the steering wheel.

He thought he'd resolved all his issues with his parents

when he 'got' est in San Diego and dabbled in Scientology, auditing that old baggage. But he knew deep down that there was some thing that traced back to Grandpa Dunn that kept him struggling to make it in his America.

"My America," he laughed, thinking of all the dead-end jobs on the phone he'd had.

Then he scoffed at his self pity, for he had made all of his choices; his parents never interfered. Another job. Another town. 'Hopes' just long enough until he ran away again to another place that brought new hope again. It always returned: failure. Each new gig gave him more experience and made him a little more jaded. He read that an American man doesn't reach his true potential until he's fifty-two. Well, even with Grandpa Dunn's money, he still hadn't made it on his own. Failure. He knew this sense of failure that others, especially women, could see. Like radar, smart women would see it and avoid him. And there were plenty of women who were no good for him; these were the women who would sink down with him until he moved on.

"Thank God I didn't marry any of 'em," he sighed. "With plenty of money in my pockets...they'll come to me now."

No more bar baggage and divorcees for this kid. Caribbean women are strong and loyal, he mused. They don't know this insane artery-clogging pace American women manifest, women who have allowed their men to speed, driving the whole country to make more.

He knew he was bitter and has lost the America he dreamed of in Oz. That's what he did with most of his time in Oz: daydream. He would have incredible daydreams up there while looking out across the verdant countryside of Jerome. Sometimes he'd rattle them off to Grandpa Dunn. Grandpa's most obvious personality trait was his patience, the way he'd pause and really listen with his whole being. It was something that made every person he knew feel important, and a trait J. D.'s father never acquired. Now J. D. realized for the first time: maybe it wasn't the million phone calls he made as the King of Slugs that made him listen--he'd inherited it from Grandpa Dunn.

The reverie ended when his digital wrist watch hit all fives at a truck stop just east of Des Moines where he gassed up, again

bought his last pack of sticks before filling himself at a salad
bar, telling himself he'd quit when he got to Jerome.

Back on I-80: it came back to him, his first night alone in
Oz. He lasted till about midnight, ending up under the covers with
Grandma and Grandpa, feeling so safe and warm and going right
to sleep.

Grandpa never remarried. I could tell he was afraid of
losing someone again. So I did my best not to give him any
trouble when I visited. Except that one time. He didn't want to
think about it after a big meal. The worst thing a boy could do to
his recently widowed grandfather was coming back to him at his
turn south on Hwy. 63 some 30 miles east on 80.

It was during a Christmas visit with his parents when he
was seven or eight. He slept in the little bedroom, the spare room
across from Grandpa's that used to be J. D.'s father's room. J. D.'s
parents were still out at a Christmas party as Grandpa slept in his
room. There was a roll-away bed his grandpa laid out every night
for his parents near the floor furnace in the little front room. In the
middle of the night, J. D. had gotten up to go to the bathroom
instead of wetting the bed, but he got lost while half asleep and
peed down into the furnace. The stench from the ammonia woke
Grandpa. He never said a word about it to little J. D., though he
had to tear apart the furnace, clean every part and put it back
together Christmas Day.

He winced at the memory of his impish deed. He lit a
cigarette and noticed the dark telephone lines and their lopsided
poles slicing past the right side of his windshield.

"Grandpa was a lineman," he muttered out loud. For the
phone company. He worked fifty years for them. "Fifty years," he
said again in utter disbelief, flicking his ash and blowing his smoke
out that two-inch space of cracked air that sucked out any trace of
smoke.

Yes, Jack Dunn had tried and failed and learned hard from
every venture he'd tried in the last thirty years. He was never
going to risk it all again to make it in America. It seemed that
when he accepted this about a year ago, staying on with
Telemaster in Omaha after three years, he began to lose that
anxiousness that was sending him to his chiropractor every week

versus every three weeks now.

"It was all fear," he reminded himself, still a good hour away from the Missouri border. When I get Grandpa's money...

He thought of the vacation in the Bahamas he'd take as soon as Grandpa's estate was settled. He'd heard from a client that a man could have his pick of a dozen beautiful native women. Then he thought: if it's that much fun down there--he'd just stay down there till his money ran out. He had nobody, and no future that required he knuckle down and work his ass off in a country that was maddened by the money chase.

Lost! He called his America.

And now he couldn't stop himself from going over in his mind all the things and places he'd sold over the phone in his America: the portable saddle rack to tack shops in Santa Rosa; janitorial supplies in San Diego; advertising in San Francisco; janitorial supplies in Phoenix; Christmas trees in Denver; satellite dishes in Omaha; long distance from Sioux Falls; chiropractors from Asheville, Manhattan and Tallahassee; home improvement in Wilmington, North Carolina; office supplies in Fredericksburg and Virginia Beach; a weight-loss diet in Bloomington, Indiana; janitorial supplies in Lincoln, Nebraska; and so many more he'd quit after a day or an hour or two. Yes, he was the King of Slugs, a numbers man, knowing if he kept dialing he'd get his sale--and he always did.

They all liked his voice and the pacing of his words--a sound that demanded to be listened to because of its truth, clarity, and direct purpose for calling. Only for one day did he work for a scam operation. It was a fly-by-night company in Scottsdale selling art paintings by a famous artist who was on his deathbed. The idea was to cash in on that. He left after an hour.

He never failed to become the top telemarketer for whatever he was selling. His tools were in his mouth, an unappreciated art form in a country that hated his kind with a passion. No matter what he was calling for, he always began his shift with the goal of not having one prospect get upset with him. Then he remembered the lead generating he did for a car dealer in Des Moines. And the living legacy he called for in California that provided a service to seniors who wanted a video of their lives for posterity. He recalled thinking of his Grandpa Dunn then, that if he could do well enough for the living legacy, he would pay for his grandfather's video and have something on his vanishing family.

The roadside mileage marker indicated the Missouri border was 32 miles away. He thought of his love life. Once for sure, maybe twice, he came close to getting married. His high school sweetheart in Kansas City, Charlotte, he dated for five years. Charlotte's the one he could've settled down with, he thought. But, he pushed her away to another who quickly put a ring on her left hand. And there was Melissa in Wilmington. She was 32 when he was 42. The sex was incredible. That fizzled out too, because she was good in bed for a reason: experience. Everywhere they went men would know her. It ended when she gave him crabs on his birthday, their last time together.

He lit a stick and smiled at the memory of shaving his moustache, eyebrows and scrotum after Melissa was out of his life. Then he inserted a tape, fast-forwarding it to the song "I Can Hear Your Heartbeat" by Chris Rea. He played it several times until he crossed the Missouri state line. He thought it darker in Missouri than Iowa.

Parking at a convenience store in Kirksville, he decided to drive straight through to Jerome and try to get some sleep half-reclined in his car on his Grandpa Dunn's property, for this would save twenty bucks. With only $590.00 to his name, he might need every dime he had if there was a waiting period for his inheritance. Getting out to stretch, he muttered: "I'm not workin' for anyone else again."

Inside the store, he wanted to get directions for the best road to Jerome, since the county road he thought he should take was closed, under construction. The convenience clerk, with his discernible Missouri drawl, told him:

"You can still take that road. Everybody drives on it after the road crew quits at four. Just drive around the barricade. It'll take ya inta Jerome alright. Not much there. Ya might miss it if ya blink," the clerk snickered.

"It's really okay to drive it?" J. D. asked.

"Sure. Everybody does. There ain't no cops on that road."

J. D. approached the barricaded road with his headlights on

high beams. He moved onto the shoulder while keeping his bright lights on and cruised 40 mph on the new blacktop that was only finished on the right lane. After a mile or so on this closed road, with only obscure farmhouse lights on both sides, he noticed the metal skeleton of a huge billboard to his right just inside a farmer's fence line. Then he saw another billboard frame. Then another. He wondered why in the hell would anyone want to advertise here. Very strange, he thought.

At the other end of the closed road was a directional sign pointing to 'Jerome, 1 mile'. On this old blacktop, he recognized a turn at the corner by the old church and cemetery that lead to Jerome's business district a few blocks away. Along the curb beside an empty lot with some kind of historical marker, he parked after deciding to walk around a bit to stretch his aching legs before going to Grandpa Dunn's to sleep. He would figure out how to get into the house after some sleep in the morning.

He could see down the cold main street an old gas station that was closed; a cafe was closed; a bar appeared open with a few vehicles parked vertically in front; a little A & P Grocery was closed. The huge lot to his right had a white cupola to the back with tall oak trees lining the back of the vast lot. He didn't remember the cupola, he remembered the trees. Behind the lot he saw a modern one-story school lit by street lights. He walked gingerly over to the historical plaque and began reading it at eye level--"Jerome School Disaster. On this site on May 18, 1927, a disaster struck this community. A madman by the name of Andrew P. Kedloe dynamited the school, killing 37, injuring 58, mostly children. We honor this sacred ground where many of our loved ones were lost."

After J. D. read the plaque a second time, his eyes bleary and tired:

"Jesus," he whispered, his breath fogging. He hobbled over to what must have been the ground where the Old School was. His first thoughts--why hadn't his grandpa or his father told him about this? Why hadn't he heard about it anyway? How could something happen like that in 1927 where Grandpa Dunn lived? That crap happens today...not then.

When he reached the middle of the lot, he stood there

stunned, his legs shivering above the cold hard ground. He then walked over to the cupola and looked at the new school two hundred yards away, then back to the ground where the Old School stood.

"Who would do such a thing?" he whispered, his words fogging the air around his face while he did the math in his head.

"Grandpa was a young man when it happened. What had he known about it since he lived here his whole life? He must've known all about it," he whispered.

Early next morning, J. D. got out from behind his wheel and stood grimacing and shivering on the frozen soil while holding his lower back and looking up at the weather-beaten boards of his old treehouse. Bleary-eyed, he tried to put his weight on the bottom step board but it crumbled to splinters. He stood back to survey the frozen branches of the large oak, its branches swaying in the stiff north wind. Just then, he turned to see a car driving by on the paved road in front of the house that was bordered by frozen cornfields in all directions, except for the ground directly across the road. That land appeared to be vacant earth not being farmed.

His red eyes scanned the old, one-story tiny house next to Oz. A faded-white paint had turned the surface to a dirty white/gray. Jack headed for the back door. He hoped it was unlocked. It was.

"I could've slept inside," he muttered while he stomped a little snow from his shoes and stepped inside the cool house.

His footsteps creaked eerily on the cracked linoleum in the small kitchen. He thought if he spread-eagled his arms, he could touch any wall from the middle of the kitchen. There was a stove, refrigerator, and a checkered yellow and white tablecloth that covered a modest table for two. He could see that the linoleum was curled at the baseboards and hammered down in places. A local bank's wall calendar hung open to March above the table. A dishrag was draped over the faucet, stiff and worn. He exited the kitchen and entered the front room.

The front room was sparsely furnished. After he stepped over the notorious floor furnace grating, he focussed on a ceramic crucifix hung dead-center on the wall. He moved slowly toward his grandpa's bedroom after opening the front room's chocolate brown curtains that were dusty and spanned the length of the small front room and offered a view of the county road in front of the house.

He touched the bedding of his grandfather's unmade bed knowing he probably died there. He picked up a framed photo of himself. It was his high school senior picture on the nightstand beside the rotary phone. How fitting, he thought. Then he went into the tiny spare room across the short narrow hallway from the bedroom. The room was filled with boxes that must hold a lifetime of things. He had a feeling that he'd have plenty of time to go through all the boxes. Just then, he heard a car door close outside. From behind a dusty shade in the spare room, he could see an old man with a thick handlebar moustache limping away from his white police car domed with a blue light. He thought the man looked like Wilfred Brimley.

"Geronimo," he whispered and smiled.

When he opened the front door, he could see that the man's limp was very painful and that his moustache hid some of the pain his mouth made with every step. He wore a flannel shirt with faded jeans. Chief Albert Linn didn't look up until he got a few feet from the door.

"Albert?"

"J. D., you look like you slept under a rock." He stepped back to let Linn hobble inside from the cold. They shook hands warmly.

"You got here pretty quick," Albert grinned, his eyes wide and clear behind his round spectacles.

"I drove in last night and slept in my car. I wish I'd known I could have gotten in."

"I'll make some coffee," Albert said, knowing his way to the coffee-maker as if he'd spent a lot of time here. But first, he showed J. D. how to regulate the old furnace by turning on the heat.

"I found him when I came by for coffee."

"Was he in bed?" J. D. asked.

"Yeah...died in his sleep."

As Albert made coffee: "I already miss him. Though I don't know a more stubborn man than he was." Albert smiled.

"Didn't he still drive a pickup?"

"He sold it a few years back when he couldn't pass his vision test."

"I s'pose you'll be stayin' here till they wrap up his estate," Albert said over coffee at the kitchen table.

"Yeah..I thought I'd sell this place..if he left it to me."

"I'm sure he did. I believe you are his only living relative." Albert handed J. D. a business card from his shirt pocket. "This is the lawyer in Hannibal who's handlin' everything."

"How long you been a cop, Albert?"

"Forty years..give or take a year. They won't let me retire. Nobody else wants the job."

J. D. wanted to mention his memory of Geronimo but didn't. "I wish I had visited him more," he said instead.

"I hear you been travelin' a lot."

"Yeah, too much I s'pose..but not much lately." An awkward pause, then J. D. continued.

"Is there a post office in Jerome?"

"In the A & P. No banks. No library. There's a bar, a cafe that serves a fair lunch; a hardware store and a gas station. And a barber shop only open on Saturday. Not much goin' on in Jerome. Hannibal's about a half hour drive. They've got some good restaurants, coffee houses, and a few clubs if ya want to meet some women. You're still single, ain't ya?"

"Yeah."

"I've been alone fifteen years now. My wife divorced me in '85."

"Sorry to hear that."

"Nah..best thing that happened to me. I was more lonely when I was married. How'd you stay single all these years? You must be about fifty by now."

"Forty-seven."

"Ah..you're still a young man. A man doesn't know what he wants till he's fifty. You know what you want, J. D.?"

"I've done pretty much what I want--travel, live in different places. I guess I'd like to have enough money to do nothin' for awhile."

Albert's eyes, the eyes of a veteran cop, looked at J. D. hard from behind smoke-colored glasses as if he was observing the similarities and contrasts to his friend, Ray Dunn.

"Your grandfather sure never spent any money on himself. Saved every dime he made for fifty years. You sure wouldn't know he had it. Never carried more than ten dollars on him. He was one man tight with a buck, that's for sure."

J. D. yawned, stretching his arms overhead.

"I gotta get some rest. I'm beat. I should've gotten a room last night."

"No motels here either."

Albert gave J. D. a set of Ray's house keys and his grandfather's wallet when they walked to the patrol car.

"My number's on the refrigerator door if you need anything, J. D."

"Thanks, Albert. I'll see ya tomorrow."

After Albert gave J. D. directions to the funeral home in Hannibal, he said, "I am glad it was you that found him. "

Albert nodded and u-turned on the patch of gray gravel that was spread without uniformity on the left side of the house in front of Oz. As he watched Geronimo drive away, he could hear his grandpa's phone ringing. He hustled to the phone in the bedroom, his legs very stiff from sleeping in his car.

"Hello..this is Ray Dunn's phone."

The caller hung up without a word. J. D. returned the receiver to the flashhook and stared with red eyes at the photo of himself on the nightstand.

Later that afternoon, J. D.'s car was parked outside a Hannibal funeral home. Inside the funeral home chapel, after having napped and showered, J. D. was wearing slacks with a sweater and tie while staring at his grandpa's lifeless body in the open casket. It's strange to see him with rouge-colored cheeks, he thought. Just then, a voice from behind startled him.

"May I help you?"

An elderly, creepy-looking funeral director appeared

apprehensive.

"I'm Jack Dunn, Ray's grandson."

"I'm sorry, Mr. Dunn. It's just that..I'm Joseph Latch, the funeral director."

J. D. felt the man's cold, clammy handshake as the funeral director continued. "I'll leave you alone with your grandfather."

"No, no, that's fine. Can we go over the schedule now?"

"If you wish."

I wish I could get the hell outta here, J. D. thought as he followed the spindly mortician into his office and sat across from his desk.

"Since your grandfather handled his arrangements well in advance, all I need is your signature to approve tomorrow's service."

J. D. signed the form without reading it.

"I've had quite a few calls inquiring about your grandfather. I've known Ray for over sixty years. He was a very brave man."

"Brave? How's that?"

"He was one of the first rescuers at the school disaster. Didn't he ever tell you?"

"No. What disaster? When?"

"The Jerome School Disaster in 1927. I'm sure you've heard about it?"

"I've read about it. Just last night."

Just then a noise coming from the chapel raised J. D. out of his chair and sent him hurrying into the chapel, stunned when he saw the back of a man reaching inside his grandpa's casket and looking for something stashed in his grandpa's clothing. J. D. rushed for the casket on the thick carpet and grabbed the man's shoulder, turning him around.

"What are you..."

J. D. froze with fear when he saw the face of a hideously scarred old man. J. D. released his grip. The scarred old man ran out of the chapel past the alarmed funeral director, who called out:

"I told you there is nothing for you here!"

J. D.'s nerves were shot as he straightened his grandpa's suit.

"I'm so sorry, Mr. Dunn. That man was one of the children

in the school disaster."

"What was he lookin' for, for Christ sake?"

"I don't know, a property deed or something."

J. D. pressed the mortician. "What deed? What's this all about?"

"Ray owned the land of the man who blew up the school."

J. D. was more than stunned as he stared at his grandpa's stone face as the mortician continued. "There's talk going around that some Hannibal businessman wants that land in a bad way."

"What is this?"

"That's all I know."

"You keep those people away from him or I'll sue your ass to hell and back!"

J. D. stalked out of the chapel, stopped at the doorway and turned back to the stupefied mortician.

"Where is that land?"

"Across the road from Ray's place."

A half hour later, J. D. entered the county courthouse in Hannibal. He entered the county Clerk's office and stood across the counter anxious to pepper the old man with questions.

"Do you know the land across the road from Ray Dunn's in Jerome? It was the land of the man who blew up the Jerome School in 1927."

No response, only a confused look from the clerk.

"I'm Jack Dunn, Ray Dunn's grandson. Can you please tell me who owns that land now?"

"You're Ray's grandson?"

"Yes!"

The clerk soon returned from the county archives area of his office toting a large register that he placed on the counter before J. D. The clerk found the property in his register, and pointed with his palsied finger.

"Robert Cochrand owns that property."

"Robert Cochrand? You sure?" J. D. queried.

The clerk turned the register around so J. D. could see for himself.

"Does he live around here?"

The clerk was aloof and didn't know the answer to J. D's question.

J. D. asked curtly, "If Cochrand owns the land, you must have his mailing address. He has to pay taxes on it like everyone else. These are public records."

The clerk remained quiet and confused until:

"Why do you want to know about that place?"

J. D. answered slowly, trying to keep his cool. "I was told my grandfather owns it now."

He squeezed the back of his neck before he showed the clerk his driver's license. The clerk turned the register back to him and flipped through pages.

"Cochrand bought both properties in 1935. He lives in Florida."

"And Ray Dunn didn't buy it after that?"

The clerk shook his head no. J. D. started to leave.

"Thank you," he told the clerk.

After he left the clerk's office, he wanted to walk down to the river. The smell of the river was taking him east and pulling him through downtown. The tourists were gone. The streets were nearly empty except for a bus blaring ahead of him till it turned, taking its noise away from J. D., leaving him with the bigger roar left unmitigated now that the bus was gone.

To himself: It's not supposed to be like this. Smooth. I want things smooth..so I can leave. What's this bull about land..across the road..and that scarred old man? Those were old scars. His eyes were terrified. Not of me. Something was there that terrified him. It'll all work out. Just get Grandpa buried..get your money..and get out.

He hadn't seen a thing till he reached the river at the front of Hill Street and saw the gray-green river flowing south. Then he could hear the river as he stepped along until his mind was calm again and he could think rationally. He turned his eyes to the west, away from the Riverboat Queen and scanned the steep hills where antebellum three-story homes stood and must have been there in

Mark Twain's day. He thought of Twain and the stories he'd read and how if not for Twain, this place would be just another river town. He remembered reading that Twain's wife called him "Youth" because of his boyish ways. Now J. D. longed for youth and the energy he would need to stay in Jerome until his grandfather's estate is settled.

Then the old idea came again: He had believed he could manifest a beautiful woman, a woman who would come to him if he only imagined her. But he could never get a clear picture of her in his mind. He always believed that when he had money it would free his subconscious to bring 'her' to him. And he knew if he thought of things like the scarred old man in the funeral home, she'd be as untenable as Missouri mist in April.

He turned back to the river and breathed deeply, closing his eyes as he kept walking, his eyes mere slits in order to keep from walking off the sidewalk. But the scarred old man came back-- those deep, horrible cuts from his forehead to chin, the chunks of flesh around the edges of both ears--gone; and those old, scared eyes staring into his--nearly made him hurl now as he opened his eyes wider to see the river to his left, across to the east bank and back again to his worn out loafers.

"Damn," he mumbled out loud. "I can't be bothered with something that happened over seventy years ago." Then he thought of his 'dream girl' and turned back, walking faster until he found a restaurant downtown to have a good meal in. He would celebrate the beginning of his new life and forget this nonsense that happened so long ago.

That night, J. D.'s empty car was parked close to his grandpa's house. All the lights were on inside the house. The Bahamas poster 'dream girl' was taped on the front room wall near the ceramic crucifix. Ray Dunn's bedroom was cluttered as J. D. opened an old suitcase of his grandfather's and found an old soft-covered book printed in 1927 entitled "The Jerome School Disaster." He opened the book to the black and white photo of the Kedloe house, where the man who blew up the school lived, across the road.

J. D. muttered his name out loud, "Kedloe."

He could see how the house looked before and after it was dynamited by Kedloe. It was white, a vast two stories, a grand house in its day; and after it was dynamited--only the blackened chimney remained.

He turned the page in the old book that had been wrapped in a plastic bag for decades. He saw a photo of Kedloe's vehicle after it was dynamited in front of the old Jerome School. J. D. knew he had to read this book from the beginning. Just then his grandpa's phone rang. He let it ring while, preoccupied, he riffed through the pages to the index and found Robert Cochrand's name listed. Quickly he went to the page where Robert Cochrand was and saw the list of the hundred-plus names of the dead and injured in the disaster as the phone kept ringing. J. D. 's trembling finger found the alphabetized name of Robert Cochrand. The phone kept ringing as J. D. flipped to another page that showed a photo of the boy, Robert Cochrand, killed in the school blast.

Finally, J. D. answered the phone gruffly, "Hello! Hello!! Who is this?"

J. D. slammed down the receiver and used more than a few expletives after the caller hung up on him.

That night in Florida, Robert Cochrand was troubled by a nightmare he'd had before. He was breathing hard during this part of the dream.

He was a young man on a beautiful morning in May at work inside his rural machine shop seven miles south of Jerome when he heard a distant muffled explosion to the north. He stopped working to listen, then continued working, unaware of what had happened in the village of Jerome where his only son and only child was being schooled.

Cochrand woke up trembling. He sat on the side of his bed in his dark bedroom, turned on the light, and took some pills from a prescription container on his bedside table with a glass of water. He then held his head in his hands and started to cry from the dream that started so long ago, but only yesterday to his heart, a heart that is thumping faster and faster like it did on his way to Jerome that day.

Next day: It's a cold day in the rural Jerome cemetery as some fifty vehicles moved slowly through the cemetery with headlights on, paying respect to Ray Dunn. After the gravesite service, a few elderly mourners made their way slowly back to the vehicles on this gray day.

Albert patted J. D. on his shoulder, leaving J. D. alone with his grandfather's floral-covered casket. Then Ashlee Jessup, a thirty-nine-year-old attractive brunette, walked over to Ray's coffin and left a bouquet of flowers on top of it. She courtesy-smiled at J. D., then somberly walked back to a new white, modified van for transporting handicapped passengers. On the sides of the van in blue lettering was "Sunnyside Retirement Village/Meals on Wheels."

Ashlee got behind the wheel of the van that was crowded with elderly Sunnyside residents/survivors of the Jerome School Disaster. Some of the survivors were badly scarred.

One of her passengers asked, "Ashlee, did he say anything?"

Ashlee answered while aloof, looking at Ray's grandson who was alone at the gravesite.

"No."

She drove the van away.

Later that day after sunset neared darkness, J. D. sat shivering on a hill overlooking the cemetery, vigilantly watching a crew of cemetery workers finish their burial detail work on his grandpa's grave.

After parking next to the Dunn house, J. D. haggardly walked over to his grandpa's roadside mailbox and pulled out a postcard addressed to Jack Dunn with only the cryptic words: "NEVER SELL THAT LAND."

Next day at noon, J. D. was awakened in his grandpa's bed

by a loud knocking on the front door. In boxer shorts, he stumbled out of the disheveled bedroom to the door. His hair was a mess when he opened the door, squinting at Ashlee's smiling face. She held a foam carryout meal container with gloved hands and wore a purple winter parka.

"Hi! You must be J. D."

J. D. nodded then pinched his eyes upon seeing the Meals On Wheels van parked beside his car.

"I'm a friend of Ray's. I thought you might be hungry," she smiled.

There was that awkward pause that two people feel who are attracted to each other, then she handed him the meal container.

"Come in," he said.

"Are you sure?"

"Yes, please."

In the front room, Ashlee removed her gloves and coat then extended her right hand. They shook hands awkwardly.

"I'm Ashlee. I hope you like fried chicken for breakfast."

"Smells good. Would you like some coffee?"

"I'd love some."

She liked his smile right away. It was a half-smile that was real and fit the lines on his face around his eyes and cheeks.

In the kitchen, J. D. didn't seem to mind that he was still in his boxers. She sat at the table while he made coffee. She had been here a hundred times; but now, it was all different somehow. She watched him open cupboards, looking for cups.

"Cups are on the right," she smiled, then got up and got two spoons from the silverware drawer.

"I don't know where anything is around here," he half-smiled.

"You keep it warmer in here than Ray did."

"Yeah?"

"He always kept it about sixty in here. I usually kept my coat on."

Coffee was ready when he returned wearing jeans, socks and a flannel shirt. She had poured them a cup and sipped at hers when he sat across from her at the kitchen table and attacked his meal.

"You make better coffee than Ray," she laughed.

"Milk or sugar?" he asked, about to stand.

"No, thanks, this is fine."

She watched him devour his meal like it was his first meal since he had arrived. It was.

"This is great," he said while chewing fast.

"You must be hungry," she smiled.

He grunted and nodded while he soaked up the gravy with a roll and finished off the chicken, mashed potatoes and green beans.

"I didn't know he had his meals catered."

"Lunch Monday through Friday. I deliver Monday, Wednesday and Friday."

"How long had he been on this service?"

"Since he quit driving."

He nodded while chewing his last bite and licked his chops like a wolf.

"You been doing this long?" he asked.

"A few years. I just do it half the year. It's volunteer work. I'm a substitute teacher at the Middle School."

"In Jerome?"

"Yes."

"Is that the school behind Main Street?"

"Yes."

"How long have you been teaching?"

"Five years as a substitute, twelve years in all."

"You live in Jerome?"

"In Hannibal."

When she got up to get him a paper towel, he really noticed her shapely figure.

"Ray was very proud of you."

"He was?"

"Yes, he was. He said you were managing a marketing company in Omaha."

Just then the phone rang in the bedroom. Ashlee seemed confused when J. D. made no move to answer it.

"Some knucklehead keeps callin' and hangin' up."

"You can get caller I. D. and find out who it is," she

suggested.

"Not on a rotary phone."

The phone quit ringing when J. D. went to the sink and cleaned his mouth and hands with faucet water, splashing water onto his face.

"You going back to Omaha?"

He returned to the table, drying his face with a dishtowel. "No, I'm gonna sell this place and do some travelin'."

"Cool. Where do you want to go?"

"The Bahamas. To be a beach boy."

When Ashlee laughed, he noticed how striking her cinnamon-brown eyes were, sparkling with health and aliveness.

"What's so funny?" he smiled.

"You don't look the beach boy type."

When she stood to remove a business card from her jeans back pocket, he again noticed her curvaceous-slim figure with long legs. She handed him her card.

He read the card: "The Country Swing."

"It's a nightclub in Hannibal. I teach country western dancing there every Wednesday night from seven to eight. It's free and lots of fun if you want to check it out."

"You're a busy girl."

"I like to stay active."

Ashlee smiled and walked into the front room . "I have a few more stops."

He followed her into the front room and helped her put on her coat.

"Thank you," she smiled.

He watched her put on her gloves. "Thanks for the great lunch. I owe ya one."

"I'd like that," she smiled.

He opened the front door for her. "Bye, J. D."

"Bye."

From the front door, he watched her drive away. His eyes were drawn to the ominous vacant land across the road. He kept his gaze on those eighty acres of black soil across the road while thinking about her eyes, and what he saw in the light of the doorway when she left. Her left eye had a pinwheeling blue speck on the upper left part of the brown; the blue speck was shaped like a flower that was exploding in the cinnamon-brown around it. They were loving eyes, like the eyes of his first love. He had seen love in a woman's eyes one time, and that one time he would never forget. He was a security guard at the entrance to the apartment complex they lived in in Lincoln. During his graveyard shift, she would come to him while he sat on a high stool watching cars come and go for eight boring hours. She was sitting on his stool in the guard shack as he stood by her. He looked into her eyes. That love in her eyes was the same color as the exploding blue flower in Ashlee's left eye--a cornflower blue, the kind of blue that's at the center of a brilliant yellow flower he'd seen in paintings in magazines.

He looked down to the business card in his hand and imagined her teaching him how to dance country western. He smiled, shook his head no, for he couldn't start something with her now. He would be gone when he got his inheritance. This craziness about the land would come out okay, and soon he would be on a beach in the Bahamas. He turned and faced his 'dream girl' on the wall. He had noticed her eyes on it for a blink that appeared to create an amusing thought on her lips that looked so sensuous to him.

He went into his bedroom and dialed the phone number on the business card Albert gave him.

"Hi, I'm Jack Dunn. Mr. Johns is handling the estate of my grandfather, Raymond Dunn. When will he be in? Next week? Yes, please have him call me. Thanks."

He returned the receiver to the flashhook cradle, then he picked up the disaster book and continued reading it where he left off.

Later that day in Ray's bedroom, J. D. was going through a box containing his grandpa's receipts and canceled checks when he found a six-month-old canceled check for fourteen thousand dollars made payable to a Hannibal car dealer. He saw written on the memo part of the check: "Sunnyside van."

He read the disaster book late into the night in bed under the bedside lamp. When he finally got to sleep, he was awakened by the ringing phone. He angrily answered the phone in the dark bedroom, and heatedly slammed down the receiver when nobody was there. He left the phone off the hook.

Next morning, J. D. was on his touch tone phone that he brought with him from Omaha. It was on the bedside table where the rotary was.

"That's right, Raymond Dunn in Jerome. Now let me make sure I have this right--as long as I have this number listed in his name, I get free local service and any services I want to add on? Good. I want to order call waiting and caller I. D."

Later that day in the Hannibal Library, J. D. looked into a microfiche viewer and read 1927 newspaper clippings about the Jerome School Disaster. A headline read: "Mad Bomber Took Revenge On a Town." He saw a black and white photo of the damaged school and the stunned locals with the words below: "37 Children Died Here When A Fiend Blew Up Their School." Next, a photo of Kedloe's vehicle after being blown apart by dynamite. Below the photo, the caption read: "He blamed townsfolk for extra school tax--so he murdered their kids."

J. D. lifted his head from the viewer and mumbled in disbelief. "Jesus."

He picked up the disaster book he found with his grandfather's things and continued reading where he had left off, becoming more and more fascinated with this true disaster.

On his way back to the Dunn house, he decided to stop at the Old School grounds in Jerome. He parked on the same spot as the night he arrived in Jerome. He walked with humble steps on the frozen soil, where the Old School once stood. His mind made him talk out loud; he could see his words fogging before him.

"I can remember bits of secret and quiet conversation my

father and Grandpa Dunn had around me. And I know now that they were consciously keeping what happened here away from me."

He stopped and looked down the cold Main Street with its downhill slope to the few businesses in this quiet village. He kept his dull-blue eyes on Main while lighting a cigarette, then he spoke slowly as if to get it all straight.

"He murdered this town. What Kedloe did seems so unbelievable. Charles Lindbergh was making his flight across the Atlantic. The Mississippi River flood was drowning this part of the Midwest. All that was going on..and this..was hardly mentioned."

Later at sunset, J. D. stood on the vacant Kedloe land across the road from his grandfather's house. He scanned the flat land of the madman who did all this, narrating to himself, as if to be sure of the facts he'd gathered.

"The night before he blew up the school, he shot his wife and dumped her body in a hogchute. Just before the school blast, neighbors heard explosions here. He had shackled his horses' legs so that they couldn't get out of his barn when he blew it up. Then the house was blown to bits. He did not want anyone else to have anything of value that he owned. God..he even sawed off his grapevines to the roots. That scarred old man in the funeral home must've been George Hammon, the most scarred of the surviving children. God, please don't let me get involved with this."

As he walked towards his grandfather's house, he wondered what his grandfather had known.

That night, as J. D. slept with his phone's ringer off, he was getting called by the nuisance caller, but now it was recorded by his caller I. D.

Next morning, J. D. copied down the phone number from the nuisance caller. He opened the disaster book to the photo of George Hammon and saw the hideously scarred face of the boy.

He found George Hammon's phone number in the phone book
and found that it matched the number on his caller I. D. J. D.
dialed Hammon's phone number and a robotic answering machine
voice asked the caller to:

"Please leave a message."

After the beep: "This is the King of Slugs. My turn." J. D.
pushed down the flashhook and dialed a Hannibal newspaper's
phone number from the open Yellow Pages.

"Classifieds, please. Yes, this is K. O. Slugs..and I'd like to
place an ad to give away some cute puppies. My number is 641-
0143 (Hammon's number). Oh! I work nights..so I prefer calls
after ten P.M. only. Yes! Great! Run it all week. When will it
run? Tomorrow if I pay today? I'll stop in today and pay cash.
Thanks. Bye."

After hanging up the phone, J. D. rubbed the back of his
sore neck while looking for a new chiropractor in the Hannibal
Yellow Pages.

Later that morning, as synovial fluid 'popped' from high
pressure side to low pressure side when J. D. got his neck adjusted
by a Hannibal chiropractor, Ashlee checked her message box in
the Jerome Middle School office and saw the message from J. D.
"My turn for lunch? Thursday at the Jerome Cafe? J. D." She
smiled at the message.

On Thursday, Ashlee entered the Jerome Cafe looking for
J. D. She could see him seated alone at the back of the cafe with a
burning candle on a table for two. He wore a tie with a blue dress
shirt and slacks, looking handsome, she thought. He stood when
he saw her approach. He pulled out her chair, helped her out of
her coat, then helped her with her chair as Jerome locals and a
waitress looked on.

"A perfect gentlemen--in Jerome," she smiled.

"A gentlemen..sometimes. But nobody's perfect."

He loved her laugh. And he really liked the fragrance she
wore. She looked so pretty in her creme-colored blouse and

matching skirt. He noticed her tiny pearl earrings and a thin gold necklace that glowed softly on the nape of her smooth neck, where he could see a beauty mark that the necklace crossed. He handed her a plastic menu.

"You sure look good," he smiled.

"Thanks," she smiled, looking up from the menu. "How'd you know I would come?"

"I didn't. I got lucky. May I suggest the chicken fried steak with mashed potatoes?" he smiled.

Again he got to hear her beautiful laugh. He hadn't really made a woman laugh in a very long time. It felt good to him, and made him think of the beautiful women he could never manifest. Could she be just one of the many to come now that I have money? he wondered. As she looked over the menu with a wry smile on her lips, he could smell that fragrance. It's not a perfume, it's some kind of oil rubbed over the skin.

He wanted to be anywhere but here with her. Though this little spot was warm and clean, it was too close to the Old School grounds. Could he find out from her if his grandpa told her anything about the disaster? he wondered.

After the waitress left with their order, she asked, "Is this what you do in Omaha?"

"What's that?" he smiled.

"Candlelight lunches in little cafes."

"Not often enough," he smiled.

"So, how's your day going?"

"Just great..now."

"How do you know I'm not involved?" she asked.

"I'm pretty good at reading things like that. I didn't think you're the type to be here if you were involved."

"And what type am I?" she asked, smiling.

He looked into her brown eyes, studying them, moving his face a bit closer to hers. "The type of woman a stranger meets in a small town, and is amazed she can go to lunch with him."

Ashlee was charmed, yet cautious. "Are you involved?" she asked.

"What do you think?"

She leaned forward to look deep into his eyes with the

flickering candle between them.
"I think..."
Just then, their meal arrived. They laughed.

After lunch, they left the cafe together. Into the cold
March wind they walked, up the small incline on Main Street
towards the Old School grounds.
"I'll walk you to the school."
"You don't have to."
"I want to. I need the exercise. I should walk more than I
do. You know any good places to go for walks around here?"
"There's Turtle Lake, a few miles north of here. It's pretty
there. Lots of trees."
"Let's walk Turtle Lake someday soon," he said.
"Okay."
"How 'bout this weekend? Saturday or Sunday?"
"Sunday afternoon."
"After church?" he inquired.
"I don't go to church," she said.
"Why don't you come by my grandpa's place around two?"
"Okay," she nodded, dipping her chin into her wool scarf.
When they reached the Old School grounds, he stayed with
her on the sidewalk versus the shortcut of cutting across.
"I've been finding out things that happened that day of the
school disaster," he said without looking at her. "I've been looking
at old newspaper articles in the Hannibal Library. It's so
unbelievable that something like that could happen back then. It
seems so unreal..like it's the kind of thing that could only happen
today with all the madness going on. So many people today are so
cold and ruthless, in a quiet sort of way. It's like they have murder
in their hearts, from being so empty. What I can't believe is that
Kedloe spent a year threading dynamite with a broom handle in the
foundation of the school. He planned it for over a year. Can you
imagine? I suppose you know all about it..teacher."
"Yeah. It has to be the worst thing that happened to this
town."
"Any town," he said.

They stopped at the cupola. He turned Ashlee around with his eyes, to look with him at the stunted Jerome business district.

"I can feel it," he said. "He killed the whole town that day. And it's still here. I can see it..by the way the town has stayed..closed, shut down, like it's stunned and can't grow."

Ashlee spoke, still looking with him down the barren street under a sky thick with deep gray layers, and those cold north winds that would blow into long gusts often.

"I see it every time I go to Sunnyside. It's on the faces of the old survivors, and when I deliver to them in their homes. Almost all of them have shown me photos of children injured or lost that day. They all seem to have pictures in their living rooms to remind them of that day. After a while, I would look away from them on purpose. They seemed to all get the message that I didn't want to hear about it every time I came over."

She wanted to say more, but stopped herself. She turned and looked at him. His teeth were shivering. She thought him handsome when he looked into her eyes just then. His smiling mouth was trembling and showing her he had had enough of such a maudlin topic after such a pleasant lunch together in the cafe. She liked the way he paused, as if to see if she wanted to leave. She listened.

"When I was in the funeral home, I caught a scarred old man looking in my grandpa's casket for something."

"Oh, no," she groaned in disbelief.

"By his age and by the looks of him, he must have been injured in the school."

"What was he looking for?"

"I don't know. I just hope the estate is wrapped up soon. You knew my grandpa. Do you know anything he might've said unusual, or anything about Kedloe's land?"

Just then the school bell rang. Her eyes told him that she had to go now.

"We can talk more Sunday," he said.

"Okay."

She hurried away from him, hustling toward the school with her low heels moving fast and pounding the cold concrete on the street and school parking area.

He watched her all the way to the school front entrance some two hundred yards away. He saw her glance back at him just before she went inside.

He lit a cigarette in the cupola before going over to his car parked in the same spot by the historical marker as when he first arrived in Jerome. He wanted to tell her about the dreams he was having in his grandpa's bed. Perhaps they would go away when he saw the attorney, he thought.

That night, J. D. slept undisturbed by nuisance calls, but the dream:

He's telemarketing nude from the treehouse. He's laughing and drinking beer while using his grandpa's black rotary phone. Then he stopped in the midst of a call, frozen with shock when he saw his Grandpa Dunn as a young man, working on a line up a telephone pole across the road near Kedloe's land.

The dream was so real that he bolted up in bed, wide awake in his grandpa's dark bedroom. Breathing hard, he lit a cigarette and smoked it while sitting on the side of the bed.

By Sunday afternoon, J. D. had finished reading the disaster book. At Turtle Lake, the weather had turned warm for this time in March as J. D. and Ashlee walked through a wooded area covered with barren poplars under a gray-blue sky. J. D. wore faded cotton jogging pants with black walking shoes, a forest green hooded sweatshirt and baseball cap. Ashlee's brown hair was pinned up under a baseball cap. She wore loose-fitting faded jeans, jogging shoes with a royal blue v-neck sweater with a white T-shirt underneath.

Squirrels scampered about them, peeking at them from behind safe places high in the poplars. He had told her about his circuitous life and all the dead-end phone jobs. She talked about her parents wintering in Arizona every year, and how happy they'd be when they returned in May looking so tan and healthy.

"You'll love the Bahamas," she said. "I was there once. It's paradise."

"I can't believe I finally get to go there. I thought it was something I'd only fantasize about till I was too old to care."

"You've really struggled being the King of Slugs."

"Yes. I'm really anxious to see that attorney. Did you ever hear from my grandpa that he owned the Kedloe land?"

"Is that what you were talking about at the cupola?"

"Yeah. That old man at the funeral home thought so. He was looking for something related to that land..a deed or something. I think that man was George Hammon..the kid who was scarred so bad from the disaster. He was the one calling my number all the time and hanging up."

"He used to come by the Middle School and walk around it like he was looking for something. Then I heard he just stopped doing it."

"How long ago?"

"It was before I was teaching there. Won't Ray's attorney know if Ray owned Kedloe's land?"

"Maybe. I don't trust attorneys. Usually when you deal with them you lose something."

J. D. took Ashlee's hand into his while they walked up a boggy knoll that overlooked the lake.

"You have such smooth hands," she said.

"My tools are in my mouth," he grinned.

They held hands as they stood at the top of the knoll at the edge of the serene lake that was gray-green and thawed in places. A cardinal stood perched atop a branch that was partly submerged a few feet from the shore.

"Isn't there something they say about seeing a cardinal in March that's supposed to mean a hot summer?" he said.

"I hope it means an early spring."

"Maybe that's it."

She felt his warm hand squeeze then let up, then squeeze again, but he didn't turn to her when she squeezed back. She waited as he looked across the lake as if he saw something interesting. It was nothing in particular. She squeezed his hand, wrapping her fingers tighter around his long, slender fingers while gazing with him across the lake.

They walked along the ridge of the knoll until he stopped and turned to her, his chin nearly touching her brow as he smiled into her eyes.

"You smell good. That sweet fragrance..what is it?"

Before she could answer, he kissed her mouth; she could taste mint and faint tobacco on his breath, but she liked his kiss, his mouth so warm on her lips, staying with the kiss, pressing with him until he went away slowly, his eyes still into hers. She hadn't been kissed in over a year and it was nothing compared to this kiss.

They walked slowly around the lake for some three hundred yards before any words were spoken between them. She was waiting for him to say anything.

"I think I'm afraid to love," he said.

"Because you're leaving?"

"No. Anytime. You're the kind of girl that should be in love."

"What kind of girl shouldn't?"

"The kind I've been with."

"They weren't school teachers who delivered meals to seniors."

"That's only part of me."

"It's that part of you I'm afraid of."

"I'm not teaching now. And that's okay. You don't have to love me. We're just friends going for a walk around the lake."

She drove him to the store and back to his house. He invited her in, but she had to run over to her parents' house to water plants and she had some papers to grade, she told him. He thought she wasn't interested in him because of the sensitive crap he told her at the lake. She thought he had lost interest when he only squeezed her hand goodbye and said:

"I enjoyed our walk. See ya soon, I hope."

She drove straight to her apartment in Hannibal; she lied about the plants and having papers to grade. She was turned off by his honesty about being unable to love, and a couple of things he told her in the car. It was the way he asked her if she liked driving the new van; and he said he had a mantra to God he began saying after his mother died: "Give me one good reason why I should believe you..believe in all the things that you send me." It bothered her the way he brought them up out of nowhere as if he was playing some kind of game with her. Like she was concealing something from him about the van. She had her reasons for not telling him Ray bought the van for Sunnyside. She would tell him when the time was right—if she had to. He was playing a game with her, and it insulted her intelligence. He'll be gone soon anyway, she told herself. But that kiss: it was incredible.

Wednesday, three days later. J. D. parked near the house and carried in a bag of groceries. At his front door he looked for a carry-out styrofoam container. Not today.

That night, J. D. entered the Country Swing Nightclub in Hannibal. He wore a faded denim jean jacket and jeans, flannel shirt with deck shoes. The music played loud from a D. J. booth. When he got a beer at the bar he saw Ashlee in her tight jeans, cowboy shirt and boots, instructing her class on the dance floor.

He sat at a table on the upper level overlooking the dance floor. She saw him and smiled. Soon, as her class danced, she went up to his table. She wanted to kiss him because she was thrilled to see him.

"I'm glad you came," she smiled.

"How'd you know I would?" he smiled.

"I didn't. I guess I got lucky. Would you like to join us?"

"I didn't come here to dance."

"Okay. I have to..get back."

He watched her shapely figure move away from him so gracefully. He stared at her while she danced with her class.

Later, Ashlee joined J. D. at his table; he was nursing his fourth beer as the D. J. blared music in the crowded club. When the song stopped, she saw him nod at the disc jockey, who began playing Merle Haggard's "That's The Way Love Goes." He stood and offered his hand for her to dance with him.

They danced close, turning slowly. He wanted to kiss her now, and knew she must be discreet here. She whispered:

"You said you didn't come here to dance."

"You were right."

"About what?" she smiled.

"It's just a walk around the lake."

She smiled up at him, putting her arms around his neck. He noticed her lips fluttered at the center as if she wanted to kiss him.

"Let's go somewhere," he said.

"Okay."

In Ashlee's apartment, later, burning candles filled the apartment as J. D. and Ashlee made intense and passionate love on the floor beside her bed. It was the first time in a long time, for each of them, that they made love.

Later the same night, naked under the covers on her bed, her head was on his chest. She kissed his chest.

"In the café..that was so romantic. I wanted to then," she smiled.

"Right there? In the café?"

"Right there in the mashed potatoes and gravy," she laughed.

Then seriously, she asked him: "When are you going to the Bahamas?"

"I'll know more after I meet with the attorney on Friday."

"I'll bet you're anxious about meeting with him."

"Yeah. This is my last shot. I've failed so many times, trying to sell some hot product or service." She kissed his neck.

"You have school tomorrow?" he asked.

"Yes."

"How long is your lunch period?" he grinned. She laughed, then kissed him.

The following day at noon, Ashlee's car was parked next to

J. D.'s car at the Dunn house. They made love on his grandfather's bed with the bedcovers strewn on the floor. In case the phone rang, J. D. set up his answering machine on the nightstand.

The Last Blanket

J. D. was seated at a large table. An attorney presided at the head of the table reading Raymond Dean Dunn's will to J. D.:

"And to my only grandson, Jack, I leave the house and ten acres of land located at the east half of southeast quarter of section eighteen in Jerome, Missouri, free and clear of any encumbrances."

The attorney stopped reading and addressed his stunned client, who had been reading ahead:

"Jack, the remainder of your grandfather's estate, for the most part, was left to you. Stocks, bonds, savings accounts, totaling nearly seven hundred thousand dollars, with the stipulation that at age fifty you will receive twenty thousand dollars a year until you reach age seventy."

J. D.'s mouth was dry; he felt like hurling as the attorney continued.

"At age seventy you will receive a sum of two hundred thousand. Jack, as you can see, there is an additional two hundred thousand dollars left to the Sunnyside Retirement Village in Jerome, to provide care for survivors of the 1927 Jerome School Disaster.

J. D. sat biting his lower lip, thinking, until he stood, slapping his copy of his grandfather's will on the table.

"This is bullshit! In three years, I'll get twenty thousand a year?"

The attorney nodded yes.

"And then when I'm seventy, two hundred thousand?"

Another nod.

"What if I die before I'm seventy or fifty?"

"If you don't name beneficiaries in your will, the state would get the balance of the estate."

J. D. sighed from frustration, running his hand back through his short hair and onto his neck, which he began squeezing while talking.

"Jesus..I don't believe this. What about eighty acres of land across the road from the house? Anything about that?"

"No, only the ten acres with the house," the lawyer said.

"I'll contest this!" J. D. barked.

"You can try. But it may be costly. I'm sorry, J. D."

J. D. began to exit the office, still rubbing the back of his neck. He stopped and faced the attorney.

"Some Hannibal businessman was interested in buying land from my grandpa. Do you know anything about that?"

J. D. left when the attorney shook his head no.

J. D. got an adjustment from his Hannibal chiropractor.

That night, J. D.'s drunk, sitting on the floor in the front room of his grandpa's house. Holding a can of beer in one hand, he stared angrily from his dream girl poster to the ceramic crucifix hanging on the wall. He ignored the phone ringing in the bedroom. He got up, wobbly, his eyes fixed on the white cross. Drunkenly he staggered to the crucifix and lifted it from the nail on the wall, about to smash the crucifix onto the floor when he saw a silver key hanging on the nail. He removed the key from the nail, returned the cross to the nail, and studied the key, turning it over, whereupon he saw the engraved number 78.

For Ashlee to sit and daydream, it meant she was caught up with all her work, including the cleaning of things she rarely cleaned. It was easy for her to drift off in her parents' backyard cupola in the little town of Thorpe, sixteen miles northwest of Jerome. She could let her thoughts come and go now. This was the place she'd go to when she was a girl of five, in the afternoon; that was when her mother took her daily afternoon nap. This was her Oz, built by her grandfather behind their second generation home.

It's identical to the cupola on the Old School lot because

her grandfather built it. He gave the cupola to the town a couple of years after the disaster.

Out here, she was truly alone, away from the antique furniture of her parents that was now covered with plastic. They wouldn't be returning in May as she told J. D. They wanted to begin staying in Arizona year round. Her father's heart was not good. They called today, telling their daughter that the Phoenix heart specialists and related care are now a priority to Mr.and Mrs. Jessup. Ashlee had to decide if she wanted to live here or sell the house.

Next morning, an elderly locksmith examined the key J. D. handed him.

"This one goes back some years," the locksmith knew.

"How old is it? Can you tell what year it was made?" J. D. pressed.

"I'd say over fifty years ago it was made."

"At least fifty? Maybe sixty? Or could it be less than fifty?"

"Couldn't pin it down for sure."

"What kind of key is it?" J. D. asked.

"It's a safe deposit box key."

"You sure?"

"Yeah, I'm sure."

"Is there any way you can find out where—what bank—or what town or state it's from?"

"The only thing I can tell ya is that it fits a Mosler Lock. Might be thirty banks in Northeast Missouri that have Moslers."

J. D. removed a pen and piece of paper from his shirt pocket. "How do you spell Mosler?"

Later that day, J. D. approached a bank manager at her desk in downtown Hannibal. J. D. sat restively on the edge of the chair.

"May I help you?"

"Do your safe deposit boxes have Mosler Locks?"

"Excuse me?"

"Are the locks for your safe deposit boxes manufactured by Mosler?"

"Yes, they are."

J. D. showed the manager his driver's license. "My name is Jack Dunn. My grandfather may have banked here. He died recently, and I have this Mosler key that fits a safe deposit box number 78. If you could please tell me if this is a key to a box he held here, I can get access through probate."

"I'm sorry, Mr. Dunn. I'm not able to give out any information regarding box ownership."

"Is Box 78 owned by Raymond Dunn? Please."

The bank manager reluctantly looked into her files.

"No."

"Thanks for checking." J. D. exited the bank.

Outside, he scanned the street looking for more banks. All day he scoured Hannibal banks with no luck.

That night, Ashlee parked her car next to J. D.'s. He sounded strange on the phone when he told her he needed to see her. At the front door of the Dunn house, she saw a note: "across the road."

She turned and saw some flickering orange light on the ground across the road on that land. She had never stepped foot on that land. She remembered being told by more than one survivor that nobody in their right mind would step on Kedloe's land, for fear he had it rigged with dynamite, even after all these years.

She crossed the road and called out to the light that was coming from an upright brown paper bag that had a candle burning inside it.

"J. D.!"

"Over here!" he returned. "There's a two by four in the ditch! You see it?"

She crossed the ditch on the board and went over to him. He was seated on the ground cross-legged, drunk and looking mean-spirited in that flickering light with empty beer cans stacked in a pyramid by the bag.

"You know how many banks there are in Missouri, Ashlee?" He paused, looking into her eyes from her knee level, his eyes wet with beer and the redness in them shone orange in the flickering light. He answered his strange query:

"Sixteen thousand four hundred and ninety-two. I ordered the entire list with phone numbers. You wanna know why?"

She nodded, getting irritated with his insolence, then he revealed a safe deposit box key in his hand, holding the key above the light coming from the top of the bag.

"I found this on a nail..behind his crucifix," he slurred. "Now..it doesn't fit a safe deposit box where he banked..or any bank in Hannibal. Now I have to call every gawd-damn bank in the state. You know why?"

Again, she shook her head no.

"Because that's where I think the deed to this here Kedloe land is..sittin' in some Missouri bank. This land shows up on county records as being owned by a Robert Cochrand. Funny how Robert Cochrand is listed as one of the dead in the school disaster. And something else that's strange. I went to the Hannibal Newspaper because my grandpa's banker said he never saw my grandpa's obituary in the paper. Come to find out—it never was in the paper! Isn't that strange, Ashlee..a man who lived his ninety-some years in this community..and no mention of his death in the paper."

Ashlee was quiet, not liking the tone of his voice. "What did your attorney say?" she asked him.

He laughed speciously. "He told me, or read to me what my Grandpa Dunn wanted in his will!"

Her eyes asked: And?

"Not a friggin' dime till I'm fifty! Then I get twenty grand a year! Oh! I do get his little shack and his ten acres around it! Your Sunnyside survivors get two hundred thousand! And they got that new van you drive around in!"

"That was Ray's idea to get the van!" she barked defensively.

She didn't like the look he gave her then, as if what she had just told him was a lie.

She continued. "He needed a tax break and he checked with his accountant."

"He didn't have an accountant!" he fired back.

"Then—his banker—or—Albert—somebody said it was a good idea for him to do it!"

"You think if I find out I own Kedloe's land it's a—good idea—I sell it?"

He could see she was hiding something, that some nerve was struck.

"He wouldn't want anybody to sell or buy this land," she said finally.

"How do you know?" he pressed.

He waited for an answer, craning his head up, watching and listening for clues.

Finally: "You really have to ask me that? You know what Kedloe did to this town!"

She'd had enough. His crooked jaw and peering eyes told her he was playing games with her. She headed for the ditch. He stood up fast, nearly falling down as he called out:

"You can save me a lot of calls, Ashlee! Tell me where the bank is! Ashlee!"

She could hear him shouting something about banks and that she ought to try calling them, then she was driving away with regrets she'd slept with him. She thought it was strange how the worst in men seemed to come out after they've been with you.

She drove toward her parents' house, not knowing why until she reached Main Street in Thorpe. There it was, that familiar landmark on the corner next to McKenzie's Barber Shop; this would be her starting point. She parked in front of the one hundred-year-old building and stared at its chocolate brown brick front that always seemed so dark and ominous at this time of night.

She looked down at her hands that were still clenched tight from gripping the steering wheel. They were still tense from the episode with J. D. on that land. She got out of her car, locked it, and began walking the three blocks to her parents' house that would be lined with ancient elm and oak trees once she left this one block area of downtown Thorpe.

Ashlee Ann Jessup just had to make this walk to her girlhood home, breathing that cold night air in her quiet little hometown. Her head was clogged with J. D.'s anger and fear she had seen so clearly in the light of that burning candle at the bottom of that paper bag. All from the loss of Ray's money, money that J. D. didn't earn, she thought, while hating something more about J. D.'s behavior tonight than what he had said. It was the innate fear a woman has of a man's wrath; she had seen it before, but couldn't recall where, as she passed by The Consignment Shoppe's window. Looking past its dark glass, she saw teddy bears partially covered with quilts, having tea with their black button eyes shining into hers under the block's only street light. This cute distraction had given her the insight she needed on this walk home. She was always the good girl and did what her family thought she should do—be a teacher, watch the house, keep the family secrets safe, and never do anything to upset things or make the family have to suffer because of my actions, she said to herself. And it came to her: That hot summer day with her father and grandfather when she was only six years old. Six, she said inwardly, because it was just before my seventh birthday. She looked up from her memory and could see she had automatically turned down Elm Street, her street, without even consciously looking. She slowed her gait to remember that day and get it over with before she entered her parents' house. Quickly, as if gassed by an ether shot into her brain cells, she could see the pinwheel of bright colors on her Grandpa Jessup's tie as her father helped his eighty-five-year-old father out of their new Ford. They had just returned from the big hospital in Minnesota. Grandpa was dying. She could remember on the drive lying on the back seat--they thought she was sleeping. Grandpa was sobbing and so was her father. She was afraid to open her eyes and let them know she was listening. They were talking about death. Grandpa Jessup was saying how it felt all these years to know he had a real reason to blame himself for the Jerome School Disaster. The sobbing coming from her grandfather was unbearable. Her father was doing his best to console him, for he knew his dying father was pleading for his own inner peace. At the time, she had no idea what her grandfather was talking about. It took her eighteen years to find out, and long after Grandpa Jessup was dead.

"I didn't know. I didn't know. I didn't know."

She could still hear her father's consoling tone while his father continued on and on. "Yes, Dad. Yes, I know. You didn't know. It's not your fault. There's nothing you could have done."

Then she remembered hearing her father sobbing with her grandfather, on the shoulder of the road when she pretended to be sleeping. She wished a thousand times she hadn't heard them that day.

As she climbed the five steps to the Jessup two-story Victorian, onto the massive cement porch, she suddenly felt compassion for J. D. and understood his behavior. He had his reasons for being angry; J. D. didn't know what the Jessups knew; or what the survivors knew; or what her friend Ray Dunn took to the grave. Poor J. D., she thought. Now it's his life too. She remembered something she read sometime after she first started teaching in Jerome. She said it before going inside.

"If you deprive a man of his dreams, you take a chance that he will eventually act out his psychotic tendencies while he's awake."

Next morning, J. D. woke up hung over; several beer cans were stacked on the bedside table. He could hear an annoying squeaking sound coming from outside. He followed the sound out to the fence on the other side of the house. There on the fence, wired to the top, was the same cryptic message burned into a piece of wood, a board two feet long and a foot tall that reads "Criminals are Made, Not Born."

It's identical to the message Kedloe left on his fence, a message telling the world "Look what you made me do."

In his boxers and T-shirt with slip-ons, he walked over to Oz and peered up at the old treehouse, then down to the ground that was beginning to soften. He knew he had a big job ahead of him. This was a job for the King of Slugs. He couldn't do it under his grandfather's roof. His grandfather's spirit and the confining space with only a view of Kedloe's land would be far too enervating, zapping the endurance he'd need for such a job.

He walked back over to the board on the fence, removed it, and flung it across the road and into Kedloe's ditch, the same ditch in which Kedloe had shot a little dog of a neighbor down the road for barking too much. Kedloe had just moved into his wife's home across the road.

By the end of the day, J. D. had replaced the steps up to the treehouse with new wood. The floor of the treehouse was good but the roof would have to be replaced by the wood and tile he bought at a Hannibal lumber yard that afternoon. The snow had really begun to melt today, he thought, as he flipped his kitchen calendar over to April. He had all the tools he'd need to do the job, even taking down the shower curtain, and he considered using the kitchen table for a desk in the treehouse when his phone rang in the bedroom. At first he didn't want to answer it, but he thought it might be Ashlee.

"Hello."

"Jack Dunn, please."

"This is Jack."

"Jack, this is Ed Stone. I'm interested in buying the land across the road from your grandfather's place."

J. D. swallowed hard, caught off guard totally by this call, the call he had hoped for.

"I think we should meet and discuss this further," he replied.

At noon the next day, J. D. nervously tapped his fingers on a table in front of a window near the Hannibal restaurant Mr. Stone had suggested.

He wore his only suit and the only tie he brought with him from Omaha. He showed up an hour early before their twelve o'clock meeting. His wrist watch had stopped, but he wore it anyway, for looks, and he checked it often during the last hour. He wanted to see this Ed Stone pull up in his car and size the man up before they met. It didn't work out that way.

"Mr. Dunn?"

J. D. turned and saw a tall man in a dark business suit that matched his dark moustache. He wore expensive glasses and gold jewelry on his big hands as they shook hands and were seated together.

"Quite frankly, I hadn't heard about your grandfather's passing until after his funeral. There was no mention of it in the paper."

"Are you from around here?"

"I live in Hannibal now. My company owns the Riverboat Queen Casino. I'm there quite a bit this time of year, getting it ready for the summer tourists."

After Stone ordered lunch and J. D. ordered only coffee, Ed Stone surprised J. D.

"Your grandfather sure didn't want to sell me that land. You know that, don't you?"

"He told me about your offer for the..eighty acres wasn't it?"

"Yes, that's right."

"What was the amount you offered?"

"Two thousand dollars an acre. A very generous offer, I thought—and still do."

J. D. blinked fast, then his eyes stayed on Stone, who could tell that his offer was more than J. D. thought it would be.

"That's about twice the value of any land around there. Why so much for that land?" J. D. asked.

"I can get commercial zoning on it and pay lower taxes out of the city limits."

"Commercial? In Jerome? There's not a main road or highway in either direction for twenty miles." Then J. D. remembered the road into Jerome on the night he arrived.

"Believe me, J. D., it's the perfect location. So—do we have a deal?" Stone smiled.

"One hundred sixty thousand?"

Stone's lunch arrived. "You won't find a better offer, J. D."

"Maybe not. I have to think about it."

"How about I call you in a week?"

"Make it two weeks."

"Good enough."

"If you'll excuse me, I'm late for an appointment." They shook hands and J. D. left the restaurant.

Outside, he headed for the river. He could see Stone's Riverboat Queen docked across the river on the Illinois side. He thought Stone was evasive about what he was going to do with the land. The longer he walked, the more he realized he had to meet with the survivors, but not through Ashlee; he didn't trust her. This time he would be careful; it was his last chance for sure. He knew he couldn't count on any money from his grandfather's estate. And then he scolded himself for not asking Stone how he knew his grandpa owned that land.

"Damn," he muttered. "Dammit!" louder when he knew nobody was around to hear him.

But what about the key to the safe deposit box. He thought he'd have to find the box before the two weeks was up. He was sure the deed to Kedloe's land was in the box; besides, he thought, I still wanna know what's in that box.

It rained for two days. The air was warm enough that all the snow was gone, washed into the Missouri water table. After inspecting his treehouse roof he decided it was time. No leaks. He used a broomhandle to run an extension cord along with the phone line along a branch that ran to the treehouse. He hauled up the kitchen table and a chair into his new office and rigged the shower curtain in place. Just then, he saw the mail carrier leave his bank list at his front door.

He was ready to make his first call to a Missouri bank from the treehouse. He donned his headset and dialed the first bank in Adel, Missouri, the first of the thousands of banks alphabetized by location.

"Who can I talk to that handles your safe deposit boxes? Thank you. Yes, this is Jack Dunn in Jerome, Missouri. My grandfather, Ray Dunn, may have had a safe deposit box number seventy-eight in your bank..thanks for checking."

J. D. called the next bank on his list after marking a letter "N" for no next to the Adel bank.

"This is Jack Dunn in Jerome. Who can I talk to that handles your safe deposit boxes?"

The battery-operated clock on his desk in the treehouse was at four o'clock. Albert parked next to J. D. 's car and limped over to the tree when he saw J. D. remove his headset and stand in the doorway.

"Now there's somethin' I've never seen—a guy IN his tree..OUT of his tree!"

Chief Linn was looking up at J. D.'s dour expression after a hundred banks told him no.

"You come here to tell me that, Albert?"

"No, I didn't. I came here to let you know that those people at Sunnyside have accepted your offer to meet with them."

Linn took a piece of paper from his shirt pocket and wedged it behind the first stepboard at the base of the tree. When he started to limp back toward his patrol car, J. D. climbed down and caught up with the old man just before he got inside his patrol car.

"Albert, are you a survivor?"

He turned and faced J. D., saying matter-of-factly:

"I was five years old, in the first grade when Kedloe blew up the school. I jumped out a window after the explosion. Then Kedloe drove up in his truck and dynamited himself in his truck filled with scraps of metal and rifle shells. A piece of the shrapnel tore into my knee. Part of it's still in there. Every step I've taken since that day has been painful, J. D. But I know I was lucky compared to some. The mail carrier had his leg blown off and bled to death in the arms of his wife right where I had been standin'."

"Did my grandpa ever tell ya he owned that land—and now

I own it?" J. D. pointed across the road.

"Kedloe's land?"

"Don't give me that dumb Columbo routine, Albert. You and plenty of other people around here know that my grandpa owned that land."

"I don't know what you're talkin' about."

He watched Albert drive away from his house. He went over to the tree and read that note that told of a meeting at Sunnyside tomorrow night at eight with directions how to get there.

Next day, the song by Love and Rockets "So Alive" played from J. D.'s car radio as he telemarketed to banks from the treehouse. Another call:

"This is Jack Dunn in Jerome. Are you the manager? My grandfather died recently and I found this key..."

Another rejection. Another call—no luck. The King of Slugs plowed on, calling bank after bank all day long until he reached the letter "C" on his list and the town with the most banks so far, Cape Girardeau. That's when he broke down and had his first cigarette of the day, then ten more before four o'clock.

7:45 that night, J. D. parked his car next to Ashlee's car and the Sunnyside van. He hadn't had a beer all day, his eyes were red and tired from calling banks all day. He kept thinking how he'd like to find that safe deposit box before he sold that land. He wore his only suit. From his trunk he got a rag and shined the tops of his black dress shoes.

The pavement was dry. All the snow was gone and soon he knew things would turn green around here in more ways than nature. He saw the image of his dream girl on his Bahamas poster as he walked confidently toward Sunnyside's front entrance. He made a mental note to remind himself to put the poster up in his treehouse for motivation tomorrow. He needed little things like that to give him a little edge for such boring work.

Inside the Sunnyside entryway, he wondered if his grandpa's money helped build this place, as he looked on the wall

for a plaque that might have his grandpa's name on it as some kind
of benefactor. Nothing. The fluorescent lights behind the
automatic doors, he knew would hurt his tired eyes. He can smell
the pungent odor of floor disinfectant, reminding his stomach that
he hadn't eaten today.

He knew his next meeting with Stone was coming up soon,
and that would give him leverage at this meeting. He knew they
would try to get to his head and emotions here; he reminded
himself that he is the King of Slugs and that things will be carved
his way. His last chance at prosperity was threatened here, so he
was prepared to be brutal if necessary.

In the lobby, he saw the pathetic eyes of a half-dozen
elderly residents staring at him from wheelchairs. They're workin'
me now, he thought, as he courtesy-nodded at their drooping
heads.

Before he reached the nurses' station, he ducked into a
restroom, where he splashed cold water onto his just-shaved face.
He looked hard into the mirror at his image. He saw the face he
used to see before getting his good job in Omaha with Telemaster.
In his tired, blue eyes, he thought back to making love with
Ashlee at her place and in his grandpa's room. It was getting
better, he thought. Then he blinked ahead to that fantasy image of
lying on the beach with his dream girl in her red thong bikini as
Love and Rockets "So Alive" played. He stayed with that image;
he could hear the music and saw her walking toward him, stopping
to look down on him on the sand, extending her brown hand out to
him. He got up and took her hand. She smiled as they walked
hand in hand along the shoreline.

He took a deep breath before he entered the partly open
accordian partition to the dining room; the nurse had just told him
the meeting was in the dining room. The first person he saw was
Ashlee, standing at the front of a group of people sitting in dining
chairs and wheelchairs. Albert got up from a group of people and
stood by Ashlee, waving for J. D. to come over to them.

J. D. felt uneasy with the elderly, scarred audience staring at him, some with twisted limbs and mangled hands and fingers. A few survivors had facial scars; they appeared to be seated at the front of the room just for the meeting.

Albert offered J. D. a chair to sit beside him at the front of the room facing the survivors. "Don't they make ya feel young?" Albert whispered to J. D.

J. D. could see that Ashlee was upset with him. He had to know why she appeared to be leading this meeting. He asked her why she was here.

"They asked me to represent them," she shot back.

"Why you?"

"Why not?"

J. D. rolled his eyes and tried not to stare at the survivors, though all of them stared at Ray's grandson.

Ashlee addressed the room loudly. "As you know, Ray Dunn left you two hundred thousand dollars to care for your needs here."

Then to J. D.: "These people want to buy the Kedloe land. Most of these people were in the school at the time of the explosion."

Ashlee pointed to a survivor in the audience. "That man in the striped shirt, he was the last student found alive in his class. Of course, he had a broken arm, cuts all over, and seven teeth knocked out. June, at the back, lost an eye and a brother. And there's Mary—she's deaf in one ear…"

J. D. lost his patience. "Okay, I get the point. What's your offer?"

"Our first offer is to have you honor your grandfather's wishes and forget about selling at all," Albert said.

The group was quiet, staring at J. D. until Ray's grandson stood, then walked over to the far side of the room. He felt and looked cornered, on the spot.

"I can't! I can't do that! I've been offered two thousand dollars an acre!"

"Ed Stone?" Ashlee asked.

"Yes."

"You can't sell that land to a riverboat gambler!" Ashlee

yelled. "Do you know or care what he plans on doing with that land?"

J. D. scanned the elderly survivors, their eyes pathetic and full of guilt in J. D.'s eyes. "I don't know or care what he does with it! My grandfather didn't leave me any money for over three years! I have a bunch of bills! I want to start a business! Now!"

More silent stares as J. D. paced the far end while lighting a cigarette. Ashlee made an offer.

"We'll give you five hundred an acre."

J. D. stopped his pacing and faced the group. "Five hundred! Look, you people—that happened over seventy years ago!"

More silence.

"What if I give you twenty thousand dollars after it's sold? Huh?" J. D. barked.

"We'll give you a thousand an acre."

J. D. nervously hit his cigarette fast while shaking his head no. "No way! No way! Get serious and make me a serious offer!"

Ashlee looked at Albert, then at the survivors as if to get their approval before she said: "Twelve hundred."

J. D. snorted his cynical reply with smoke and left the room. Albert called out to him.

"Think about it, J. D.!"

It rained hard the next day. His dream girl poster was on the treehouse wall in front of him as he finished calling another wrong bank and marked "N" next to it on his list. The shower curtain was drawn shut so water didn't leak into the treehouse. He dialed another bank from his list.

That night he was dead tired and went to bed early after a few beers and after counting his dwindling money. He hadn't slept well last night after the meeting at Sunnyside. He was snoring by nine o'clock and having his most vivid dream by midnight.

In his dream, he could see his eighteen-year-old Grandpa Dunn sitting at a table by a kerosene lamp in a small room. He was writing a letter with considerable thought and energy pouring out of him. Then it was a beautiful spring day. Young Ray Dunn was wearing a hard hat and utility belt while working up near the top of a telephone pole. There is an envelope sticking out of his back pocket. Just then, on the sidewalk below young Ray, a young and attractive school teacher walked by and smiled up at Ray. Ray was smitten with the young teacher. Ray had to say something to her.

"Teacher! Can I come to school today?"

She turned and saw Ray's smiling face. She smiled back at him and continued on, entering the old Jerome School. Ray removed the envelope from his back pocket and looked intently at it as if weighing whether or not to give it to the teacher. He put the envelope back into his back pocket and continued working on the telephone line.

J. D. woke up after his dream. He paced the room while he smoked a cigarette in the dark bedroom.

Next day, J. D. eliminated more banks on his list from his treehouse office. Later on, he got his phone bill and was afraid to open it; it lay unopened near his phone until later in the afternoon. The two hundred and fifty dollar phone bill would eat up most of the money he had left to his name. He dialed a phone number from his address book.

"Mr. Stone, please. Jack Dunn."

While on hold, J. D. saw another car drive slowly by his house then pick up speed. Ever since the meeting at Sunnyside, this kind of thing happened often. When Stone came on the line, he asked J. D. if he had made a decision regarding his offer.

"I'm considering another offer," J. D. said.

"Better than two grand an acre?"

"No..twelve hundred."

"I don't understand."

"My grandpa gave a retirement home in Jerome two hundred grand. They want to buy Kedloe's land for as little of that money as possible. Those people are survivors of the Jerome

School Disaster. So—it's been pullin'at me."

"I see. I've been down this road with your grandfather. I tried to convince him that Kedloe's land should be used to help the economy in Jerome. The worst thing that could happen to Kedloe if he were still alive would be Jerome profiting from his land. J. D., I'm going to have a meeting with an associate today. I know you're going to like what we have to offer. How 'bout I stop by your place tomorrow..say..after one?"

"I'll be here."

After talking with Stone, he looked over at the land across the road, whereupon a diminishing smile left his face. He went back to his list and called the only bank in Drexel, Missouri; he struck out again, and again, and again, sixty-seven times until he left the treehouse and took a long nap.

That night, he laid in bed an hour before going to sleep. He thought about Albert, Ashlee, and the survivors too much. But when he did finally get to sleep, he slept throughout the night without dreaming about anything that he could recall.

Next day at one o'clock, Stone and J. D. were having coffee in the Dunn kitchen, both standing on the space where the table used to be. When J. D. raised his coffee cup to his lips, Stone could see J. D.'s hand tremble, and his eyes were red with dark circles under them from thousands of fruitless phone calls and money worries. The King of Slugs was stressed out. When Stone sipped his coffee, J. D. thought how his guest resembled the actor Dabney Coleman.

"I probably know more about that disaster than anyone," Stone said with confidence.

"Then you can understand why I'm considering the lower offer."

"You bet I can."

"How do you know for sure my granddad owned that land?"

"I had a title search done ten years ago."

"Robert Cochrand owns it..according to county records."

"Robert Cochrand, that's right. He was a student killed in the school explosion. Did you know his father's name was Robert Cochrand?"

J. D. shook his head no while he listened intently.

"Cochrand Senior lives in Florida. He must be about a hundred years old. Your granddad and Cochrand became friends after the disaster."

J. D. went over to the kitchen sink counter and leaned against it. "How do you know all this?" he asked.

"I spent a small fortune finding out. See, Robert Cochrand the boy, the one killed in the disaster, was never named Robert. His birth certificate lists his real name as Bobby..not Robert. Old man Cochrand agreed to use his name as owner of the land but never actually wanted to really own it. They knew what they were doing—taxes paid by a blind trust every year and friends in the courthouse listed a bogus grantee as Robert Cochrand so nobody knew when the land was bought or how to find Robert Cochrand. Anyone from around here didn't want that land anyway for fear Kedloe still had the place rigged with buried dynamite. Nobody would turn up that soil."

Stone , in his expensive business suit, went over to his briefcase on the counter and opened it. He took out an envelope and handed it to J. D.

"That's a general warranty deed that shows you are the current owner of Kedloe's eighty acres."

"So this means I don't need to find the deed?"

"That's right. You are the heir in probate, the only heir."

J. D. thought of the wasted calls he made to all those banks; then, the thought hit him—what's in the safe deposit box?

Before he could dwell on that: "What if my grandpa sold the land to someone else in the last ten years? You said ten years ago you ran a title search."

"I ran another one after our last meeting. That's a current deed, and here's a contract with my final offer of two hundred thousand dollars."

J. D. is stunned to see the check for two hundred thousand.

"And the retirement home can keep their money," Stone

smiled.

"That's…"

"Twenty-five hundred an acre," Stone said.

J. D. started to pace around the kitchen. "Twenty-five hundred," J. D. muttered. "Why wouldn't he just leave the land to Sunnyside?"

"I don't know what your grandfather's thoughts were. All I know is this offer stands until I leave this house."

"I have to accept it now?"

"Or decline now."

"Twenty-five hundred an acre?"

Stone nodded yes while smiling. Then J. D. asked:

"You really want that land in a bad way, don't ya?"

"We have to begin construction now to be open for business this fall."

J. D. stopped pacing. "What if Sunnyside matches your offer?"

"Would you take their money..or mine?" Stone said.

J. D. paced into the front room. He looked at the crucifix on the wall; then, he looked at the blank space where his dream girl poster was before returning to the kitchen. Stone's eyes wanted an answer.

"Okay, where do I sign?" J. D. said.

Stone smiled and pointed on the contract after giving J. D. a pen.

"Sign here and..here."

After signing away the Kedloe land, J. D. sighed, "I'm glad this is over," J. D. sighed.   "Me, too," Stone agreed.

They shook hands after Stone gave J. D. the check for two hundred grand. Both seemed happy with the deal.

After Stone left, J. D. opened his bare kitchen cupboards. He'd been eating out of cans and living on popcorn and beer. He was close to going to a title exchange loan company, getting some cash for his car in order to pay the big phone bill. His eyes moved down to the big check in his hand. This was his ticket. His hunger was over, yet he knew the scorn coming from the old Jeromites would be harsh and heavy when they found out he'd sold the land of the most evil man they had known.

He could not leave town right away. He had to sell this place, and what about the key? he thought.

He walked into the front room and stood in front of the hanging crucifix, removing it from the nail. He looked at the key on the nail, squinted at it, trying to squeeze out some vision of what that key unlocked. Then, he flashed to the letter in the dream, in his young Grandpa Dunn's back pocket. What were those words his grandfather penned with such fervor? There had to be something in that box, something important. Could he run away with his money now and let a realtor sell this crackerbox?

"What should I do?" he asked the cross in his hand. "Show me what to do. I know I'm of little faith and pursue my self-centered dreams. But that's who I am. If you show me what to do, I'll do it. Just show me."

He returned the cross to the nail, covering the key. Then he went back into the kitchen and picked up the check from Stone on the counter. He wondered why even now that he had more money he still felt half-alive. This was more money than he thought he'd ever get from his inheritance. The money felt like a new weight, a burden he knew he'd carry everywhere he went.

He lifted his tired eyes to the light above the dusty yellow cloth curtains above the sink. The floor of Oz was visible and his dream girl imagined. The rush of wanting to drive into Hannibal and deposit his big check was gone.

He climbed up to his boyhood retreat, donned his headset, smiled at his dream girl and dialed the First National Bank in Edna. He noticed his voice was more powerful, and he could tell that the strain of its sound was diminished considerably. Bank after bank said no, that number seventy-eight was not owned by Raymond Dunn. He called another bank, then another, and another. This went on for an hour or so.

J. D. walked into his grandpa's bank in Hannibal, the same bank where he kept his dwindling checking account. He wanted the bank manager to handle his deposit. He told the manager he wanted a favor or he would find a banker who would.

After leaving the bank, J. D. went straight to his chiropractor and got an adjustment. His chiropractor knew a real estate agent who would sell his house fast. J. D. called the agent from the doctor's office before having dinner near the riverfront, where he could see Stone's riverboat across the river.

J. D. took the day off from calling banks. He spent the morning with the real estate agent, who planted a "For Sale" sign in front of the Dunn house before he left. As the agent drove away, Chief Linn and Ashlee drove up in Albert's patrol car. He could tell they were upset with him. He started to walk toward his front door, but they hurried and caught up with him. J. D.'s back was to Albert when Albert yelled at J. D.

"I told everybody you wouldn't sell for no amount of money! But a friend in the bank told me he saw a check for two hundred thousand dollars from Ed Stone!"

J. D. turned and faced them. "I sold it. It's over!"

"That's what you think, buster! It's not over by a longshot!" Albert shouted, his face red.

"We would have matched Stone's offer, J. D.!" Ashlee cried.

"You had a chance to match his lower offer! But you keep your money! I'm sure my grandpa didn't give you two hundred grand to give to me!"

"You don't know anything!" Albert roared.

"I know exactly what he was doing!" J. D. yelled. "And you two are good at it like he was! It's called withholding! He's even withholding now—until I'm fifty! My father used to always tell me how his father was always gone..workin' sixteen hours a day—saving his money—and for what? My father passed the same thing down to me..nothing! And now..now that I'm at the age when I have tried enough things to know what doesn't work, all I need is money! The money is my father and grandfather! And I'm not waiting to get it! When this place is sold..I'm outta here! You keep your money and give it to your little friends in your little banks with their little minds..and you watch your little town die!"

"That Ed Stone is bad news, J. D. He's all money and no heart. He's got bad plans for that land," Albert warned.

J. D. turned and headed for his front door. Albert cried out to him.

"J. D. In ten, fifteen years, we'll all be dead and you can sell then!"

Ashlee and Albert pressed J. D. to his door. J. D. fired back at them after he opened the front door. "It's sold!"

"You can say he used duress and give him back his money!" Ashlee cried. "J. D., we'll give you the two hundred thousand!"

He went inside his house and slammed the door shut. From behind parted curtains he watched the patrol car leave his drive. Then he looked across the road at the land he sold, mumbling:

"It'll be alright."

That night, it took J. D. a while before he got to sleep. At pre-dawn, he was into a more vivid dream of the same scene where young Ray is working on the same telephone pole after the young teacher entered the school. It's a beautiful spring morning. The letter is still in young Ray's back pocket when there is a great dynamite explosion that nearly knocks Ray off the pole. He held onto the pole for dear life.

J. D. bolted up in bed, breathing hard from his dream. He got out of bed, lit a cigarette and nervously paced the dark bedroom until he turned on the bedside lamp, hurriedly found the disaster book and feverishly riffed through the pages until he found what he was looking for. He saw the black and white photo of the same teacher his grandpa liked; she was the same teacher in his dream. He quickly read in the book that her name was Mary Chatman, one of the teachers killed in the blast. She was found in the rubble with her arms around two dead children who were her students. Just then, coming from outside the house, he could hear the sound of loud engines approaching. He ran to the front room window, parted the curtains and saw a long row of headlights from

a construction fleet of trucks, graders, and other earth moving
vehicles entering onto the land across the road. He stared intently
at the procession of heavy machinery knowing something was
wrong with all of this.

      Later that day, by late morning, J. D. had called another
twenty-five banks above the roar of the very large construction
crew leveling Kedloe's land. He kept his curtain closed in Oz to
mitigate some of the background noise, but he had to yell at every
bank representative on every call. The calling was a bit easier, for
he had asked his banker in Hannibal to e-mail every bank in
Missouri, telling them he was looking for the owner to Box 78 and
that he'd be calling them soon to verify ownership.
      After another bank call, he heard a familiar voice coming
from the base of Oz.
      "J. D.!" Albert called out.
      J. D. opened his curtain and saw Albert with a rolled up
newspaper in hand.
      "You read the paper today?" Albert called up to him, then
walked away after wedging the paper behind a step-board. He
watched Geronimo drive away fast, then he climbed down, opened
the newspaper, and read a shocking article on the front page titled:
"Developer Plans Missouri Madness in Jerome."
      "Developer Ed Stone revealed plans to rebuild mass
murderer Andrew Kedloe's farmhouse on Kedloe's land. Stone
plans to market the rural Jerome site as a bizarre tourist attraction
scheduled to be opened by this fall. A Jerome Township meeting
will be scheduled soon, Stone said, adding, he is not interested in
purchasing the Jerome Old School grounds currently owned by
Jerome Middle School teacher Ashlee Jessup. Stone said he
knows the township council would never allow the Old School
grounds to be part of Missouri Madness. The riverboat casino
owner plans to shuttle his tourists by the Old School, pumping
millions into the Jerome economy, which is why Stone is confident
his project will be approved by the township council."
      J. D. finished the article, dropped it to his waist and stood

watching the construction crew busy at work. To himself he mumbled:

"Jesus."

J. D.'s dream came around two in the morning that night. The scene was the same, but the characters had changed: Instead of young Ray writing the letter by the kerosene lamp, it was J. D. of today who was writing with passion. Then it was J. D. working up on the telephone line with the letter in his back pocket when the school was dynamited. Hanging on for dear life after the explosion, J. D. was soon digging furiously in the rubble of the school, where he found the dead teacher, who was now Ashlee Jessup.

Ashlee was asleep when she heard the loud knock on her apartment door at 3:30 A.M. She put on her robe, turned on a lamp by her door and peered through the peep hole at J. D.'s messy-haired countenance.

"What do you want?" she asked from behind her locked door.

"I have to talk to you."

"Go away."

"Ashlee..I'm not leaving till I talk to you..Ashlee..please."

She let him in. They stood near her door; she had her arms folded in front of her, not happy with her visitor.

"I know you think I'm a dirt bag. Stone offered me two hundred thousand and I took it. I didn't know what his plans were until I read today's paper," J. D. said.

"As if that would have made a difference," she said cynically.

"Why didn't you tell me you own the school land?"

"The survivors bought it and named me trustee. Now will you go, please?"

She started to close her door when J. D. removed the disaster book from his coat pocket and showed her the photo of the young teacher in his dream who was killed in the school explosion.

"Did you know her?" he pointed.

"No."

"That was the woman my grandpa was in love with."

"Why are you showing it to me?"

"I don't know..I..they can still stop this at the council meeting."

"Stone's bought them like he's bought you."

He went to a 24-hour restaurant, ate a big breakfast and had smoked a dozen cigarettes by the time the morning paper headline told him "Say No To The Madness." It was an article he knew Ashlee, Albert and the survivors had composed. The Jerome council meeting would be on May 15th, a Saturday that would be just a few days before the 73rd anniversary of the disaster.

He thought about leaving town before the meeting. After waiting in his car for over an hour for a grocery store to open, he had decided to go ahead and stock some food, continue pounding his bank list, and see what happens. If the house sold fast, he'd hang out in Hannibal, he thought.

In the hallway just before exiting Ashlee's apartment building, this 'thing' or feeling came over him and stayed with him as he sat in his car waiting for the store to open. It was all these little things he'd been hating about his America since the 1970s. It was becoming clear that it was all part of the duality Stone's money could give him: the prosperity America promised; and the brutal plans Missouri Madness would deliver in buckets of fear and hate and misery to the masses.

He wanted to race back over to her apartment, kick down the door, and hold her arms to her sides in her bed while he poured out his thinking. He would make it all right with her if she could only understand this 'thing' about his America that made him sell out to Stone. He began to talk in the car, pretending she was there in the car listening to him.

"Stone bringing back Kedloe is no different than America's state and federal cruelty for letting her habitual criminals back into society. It keeps the fear level up. Fear is big money in America. Attorneys make big money defending and prosecuting these repeat offenders. Repeat customers. Insurance companies live on fear. And so does the media. It's all fear!" he screamed.

Then he talked softly, about how public schools teach children things in books and on computers that have nothing to do with how we live together.

He stopped talking and imagined what she would tell him now. He could hear her telling him that nobody would know who Kedloe was, except for the locals and the few survivors left in Jerome. Now, thousands more will know what your grandpa wanted kept hidden from the public.

Then he felt a knot in his gut, for taking Stone's money and making this Kedloe madness real for him, and soon, thousands more would know this world was not so safe back then, or any better than it is now.

"God, what have I done?" he screamed.

On his way in to the store, he knew it was the dreams that were keeping him here. And now, he had money, Stone's money. He didn't have to run away like a hundred times before in search of a better job. He had a job.

He pounded the phone from Oz like gangbusters all day. The weather was beautiful; the greens of spring were filling-in more each day. His last call ended the same as the others.

"Thanks for checkin'."

He looked down at his list after marking off the bank in Hartville. He had so far to go—if the town is at the end of the list, he thought. He removed his headset and turned his head to see Stone's crew already laying pipe and digging and surveying as if the council approved it. Maybe Ashlee was right, he thought. Then he noticed something about being on the phone today: ever since the grocery store this morning, he'd been talking out loud to himself. Even between calls, he was ranting about the work going on across the road.

"I'm going mad," he said.

He stood, staring at his poster. He paced in a tiny circle as if in a cage, the creaking wood under each step inaudible because of the roar of machinery on Kedloe's land. He picked up his pack of cigarettes on the table and crushed them in his hand, declaring above the din:

"I quit!"

"Not you, you bastards," he said to his bank list. "Smokin'..I quit!"

He sat down, donned his headset and dialed another one-bank town in Hayti.

Friday, the banks kept saying no, and he kept saying no to nicotine. His energy level was up. And no more beer. Alcohol only made him crave smoking more. He began to eat more since his appetite increased. He was conscious about staying away from junk foods. He wanted to be in good shape when the house sold and he took off to find his dream girl. That is, if the council rejects Stone. That damn meeting kept creeping into his mind. What will I do if that place is approved? he thought a thousand times.

May 15th, Saturday night. A large cluster of vehicles were parked near the small building adjoined to the one-stall fire station as J. D. parked his car near Ashlee's car. He caught himself muttering while heading for the dark-brick structure, grumbling about how they better shut down Stone so he could get outta this friggin' town.

The meeting was about to begin. Not many in the room paid much attention to the man who sold the Kedloe land as he took his place on a folding chair at the back of the room. He could see the glum faces of the township council looking guilty as if they had been bought by that snake oil salesman Ed Stone in the slick suit sitting next to an associate at the front of the room. Albert was in uniform as if to stop any trouble; he was seated beside Ashlee and survivors from Sunnyside, some in wheelchairs. Albert looked at his watch and got up to address the room.

"You know why we're here. We'll listen to what Mr. Stone has to say..then the Charter Township will vote on it."

Stone stood facing the room in front of a large table that had a purple cloth over it. "Missouri Madness will bring growth and prosperity to Jerome. The research and stats are in. Forty new jobs for township residents. Business for township businesses! All because my company created a part of Jerome's history..a history that is terrible..but public domain!"

Just then, a hush came from the room, not from Stone's pitch, but the old man with the cane, Robert Cochrand from Florida, who sat down next to J. D. at the back of the room as Stone continued.

"I have created a part of your history that thousands of people will pay to see today!"

Ashlee called out from her seat. "Don't you think this is crude and distasteful, Stone? Many people here—"

"Many people will approve of this if the community benefits!" Stone interrupted.

Stone removed the cover from the table model of the Kedloe farm, causing gasps from some of the survivors as Stone continued.

"Seventy-three years ago, Kedloe destroyed Jerome! And he did a helluva job! Yes, I'm an outsider! But I know a goldmine when I see it! And there's only one way to get that spineless bastard, Kedloe! Make money off Kedloe's land and name! Some of you older folks know that nothing would tick off Kedloe more than to know he is responsible for a new twenty-four room wing at Sunnyside!"

Stone's associate handed Stone a rolled-up set of blueprints of the Sunnyside addition.

"Yes!" Stone continued to the confused survivors. "In the very same town he tried to destroy!"

The room stirred with this news, but Ashlee didn't buy into it. "You have no right to do this, Stone!"

"This is good!" Stone pointed to the blueprints. "You know Kedloe sure as hell wouldn't vote for this! Yes, a tourist attraction that is a part of our past and a part of American history! Admission will be ten dollars for adults, children under sixteen free, accompanied by an adult! Two dollars from every admission goes to Jerome!"

"You can't have kids in there alone!" an audience member blasted at Stone.

"No one under eighteen will be admitted without an adult!"

Stone pointed to the model. "The tour will begin in the farmhouse, then to the other buildings! 1920-era school buses will shuttle the tourists past the Old School grounds where they will see a video on the bus about the disaster, focussing on survivors and rescue workers mainly!"

"No way, Stone!" a voice in the audience barked.

"Let me finish!" Stone insisted. "The tourists will be encouraged to visit Jerome businesses! That's why part of this project will be to restore businesses on Main Street!"

"Who pays for that?" a man asked.

"Whoever wants to prosper! Now look..we'll fix-up the streets, sidewalks and lamp posts! But the way most of the storefronts look now, anything is an improvement!"

A resident barked his question to Stone. "What makes you think anybody wants to see that?"

"I'm a gambling man, and I'm betting on it."

"What about the people that went through that? Ashlee asked. "They don't want this going on all over again! Don't you see that?"

Stone handed the council members a stack of papers before answering. "For over ten years, I've been getting feedback from Jerome residents! You'll see that a vast majority will tolerate this project, if the community will benefit. I think the council is ready to vote on it!"

Ashlee could tell the council was with Stone. But just then, elderly Mr. Cochrand stood and walked gingerly with the aid of his cane, up to Stone and his project model. Cochrand turned and faced the audience. All were quiet, listening; they could see the pain on the old man's face as he spoke to the room.

"You people come from good stock. That's why it was possible for most of us to heal after our losses. We had a hard time getting our medical bills paid..and high-risk insurance premiums prevented good jobs for many of you. This country takes better care of its criminals! White collar crooks like HIM go on making money off our pain!"

Cochrand turned to Ed Stone in the quiet room. "You have NO RIGHT to do this!"

Cochrand started swinging his cane and whacked the model of Kedloe's place. Albert intervened, stopping Cochrand from swinging his cane. The old man was exhausted, breathing heavily while he clutched his chest. Ashlee helped Albert escort Cochrand out of the room as the guilty-looking council voted on Stone's project. Albert came back inside after helping the old man into his rental car.

Ashlee watched Mr. Cochrand as he rested on his back on the back seat of the rental car. His breathing was calming some. When she returned inside, the vote was over. Albert had read the passed proposal for Missouri Madness to a stunned room of survivors and their families. As Stone and his associate were beaming with the news while repairing the damaged model, Ashlee went over to Stone.

"You bought those votes like you bought that land."

"Sore loser?" Stone smiled.

"Go to hell."

Ashlee saw J. D. had left the room. She hurried outside to catch up with him at his car. "J. D.!"

He turned back to her before opening his car door. "Now you can watch what you did..and live with it," she said, then, he got in his car and drove away.

Albert followed Ashlee as she drove the somber survivors back to Sunnyside in their van. Albert saw Cochrand's rental car in the Sunnyside parking lot. He checked to make sure the old man wasn't yet inside the car. He wasn't. Albert helped Ashlee escort the survivors back to their rooms; that's when a nurse on duty told Ashlee that Sunnyside had over twenty calls from people wanting to know if Stone's project passed.

Albert saw Cochrand sitting in a private room talking to one of the resident/survivors and old friend, Bill Dixon.

"Something has to be done to stop this nonsense," Cochrand groaned to the bedridden Dixon.

"I don't know what you can do now," Dixon said.

"Got any dynamite?" Cochrand joked.

Dixon chuckled. Just then, George Hammon, the most scarred survivor, entered the room wearing a baseball cap pulled down over his eyes. Hammon closed Dixon's door behind him, since he'd seen Chief Linn in the hallway. He stood at the foot of Dixon's bed after shaking hands with the visitor from Florida.

"Got any dynamite?" Dixon asked Hammon.

Hammon laughed, but then added seriously: "Wouldn't do any good now anyway. Let 'em build it first."

"Count me in," Cochrand stammered.

"Were you at the meeting?" Dixon asked Hammon.

"No. I stayed clear of it. I knew they'd approve it."

"Too many gone now," Cochrand said.

Hammon and Dixon nodded in agreement. "I was talkin' to a grandson of Ellen Hunt. You remember Ellen Hunt?" he directed at Cochrand.

"Who?" Cochrand asked feebly while he leaned closer to Dixon.

"Ellen Hunt! She lost part of her foot in the explosion! She was Eddie Hunt's sister!"

"Oh, yes, I can recall her," Cochrand said, his eyes glowing from his heart medicine.

"Her grandson said he'd vote for it! Cause he said it would help his business! He's got that Dairy Queen down by the crossroads!"

Cochrand didn't hear much more or care about what was being said between Hammon and Dixon. He had to start his drive for St. Louis to catch his return flight. He knew his nurse would come after him if he didn't show. Dixon and Hammon thought it odd when the old man just left the room without saying goodbye.

"He didn't want to be here on the eighteenth. I know that much. He's never returned for any of the reunions. If we were organized, this wouldn't happen," Hammon remarked to Dixon.

"You can't blame him. Everyone handles their grief their own way."

Hammon nodded, was silent for a few moments, then:

"Ray Dunn sure wouldn't approve of this."
"No..no..that's for sure," Dixon agreed.

That night, J. D. was awakened by heavy traffic outside, and now a new light was on, shining wide shards of white beams across his bedroom ceiling. He opened the front room curtains by pulling down hard on the curtain runner string. He could hardly believe what his eyes were seeing. Stone's crew had installed night lights so his crew could now work 'round the clock. He could see the lumber from trucks being unloaded, then quickly hoisted into place. This was the beginning framework for the Kedloe farm that was now being hammered, pounded and sawed into place. Then he saw a portable guardshack delivered and a crew set to work on it, setting up power and phone lines to it.

The King of Slugs raked both hands through his messy hair and squeezed the back of his sore neck. He craved a cigarette now, but said no, and paced for twenty minutes before going back to bed with his bedding pulled over his head and balls of cotton stuffed in his ears.

Next day, it rained all day and the crew stayed home. Stone pretended to be sensitive and closed down construction until the 19th, observing the anniversary of the disaster and even announcing his good deed to the media in order to mitigate survivors' reactions who were returning to Jerome because of Missouri Madness.

Ashlee drove by in the Sunnyside van. She looked at the treehouse even though it was Sunday. Traffic was getting heavy around here, curiosity about this Missouri Madness was giving Stone what he wanted and twenty-six billboards on every major road within two hundred miles of Jerome were responsible for some of this increased traffic around sleepy Jerome.

Ashlee heard that Marian Hunter, an eighty-eight-year-old survivor, wanted to move into Sunnyside soon, but wanted to know how the food was. Marian, a widow for thirteen years, didn't drive, and she had just been released from a Hannibal hospital after falling down in her bath and cracking her hip. Ashlee was asked by Sunnyside staff if she could bring her by for a visit to Sunnyside after a catered Sunday dinner.

She was five miles away from Marian's house in Bordon, Missouri, as the elderly widow watched for Ashlee from her rocking chair on her front porch. Marian was terrified of going into Sunnyside. This fear brought back a memory of when she was a girl returning to her school about a year after she's had her left leg amputated three inches below her knee. She was one of the children who lost a limb in the disaster. She remembered how friendly and helpful everyone was, and how the Jerome children never stared at her like in other places. But this one day in the Jerome school, there was a thunderstorm overhead. She would never forget the terror mixed with compassion and understanding they all shared for that brief time. It was a beautiful moment then and now for her as one student then another began to cry and soon run out of the classroom. All ignored by the teacher and her classmates. All ignored.

Marian saw the new Sunnyside van coming down her driveway, the dry gravel crunching under tires. She could see the pretty teacher from Jerome smiling at her while walking toward her house carrying the styrofoam container with both hands extended in front of her. Just then, another vehicle pulled in and parked behind the van. Ashlee continued toward Mrs. Hunter after she saw J. D. get out of his car. He looked a mess in his three-day beard, and his clothes were wrinkled as if he'd slept in them. Ashlee handed the container to Mrs. Hunter in her rocker.

"I hope you like pasta," Ashlee smiled.

"Oh, yes, I do. Are you the Jessup girl?"

"Yes," Ashlee smiled.

"I knew your grandfather and your father."

"Really?"

"Oh, I should say so."

Ashlee knew she had to stop the flow of this conversation, not liking where it was headed because J. D. was listening.

"Hi," he smiled at Mrs. Hunter while he stood just a few

feet behind Ashlee.

"Hello," Marian smiled.

"I'm a friend of Ashlee's. My name's Jack Dunn."

"You must be Ray's grandson."

"Yes, ma'am."

"Isn't it just awful what they're doing there?"

"Yes, it is," he agreed, looking sheepishly away from Ashlee's cold stare.

"It was your grandfather who rescued me out of the school rubble. He was a very brave man. The wall was about to collapse on him any minute. But he stayed right there digging until he got me out."

Ashlee spoke coldly to J. D. "After Mrs. Hunter has her lunch, I'm taking her to visit Sunnyside."

"Maybe you could stop by after your visit. I'd like to talk to you," he told Ashlee.

Ashlee turned back to Marian, who was now getting up to go inside her house to eat her meal. Ashlee took the food container from her.

"Not today," she answered J. D.

He pursed his lips, nodded, and went back to his car.

He couldn't stand it on the 18th of May. While on the phone hammering banks, the traffic going by on the front road was bumper-to-bumper, hundreds and hundreds of gawkers. He slammed down his headset on the table and looked across the road at the guardshack. He could see a uniformed security guard smoking in front of his window at the front of his perch. Though the construction was shut down for today, the slow-moving vehicles and their eerie silence was more of a distraction for him on the phone.

Wednesday night, J. D. exited the Country Swing after the bartender told him that Ashlee quit teaching dance there. He drove over to her apartment in Hannibal, but she must have moved out, for he noticed her name was not on the mailbox.

Two days later, the pace to rebuild Kedloe's farm was furious. Day and night the crew worked on a deadline—to be open by the 1st of June for summer tourists. It was so loud across the road, the King of Slugs had to keep one finger over his ear in order to hear bank after Missouri bank tell him "no." He had reached the letter "K" on his list, thinking this might be it, all because of Kedloe. But then, he jumped ahead on his list and called Kedloe's hometown in Tecumseh, Missouri. No luck.

That afternoon after school just let out, he sat down quietly on one of the student desks in the back row of Ms. Jessup's classroom. Ashlee had her back to him and didn't hear him enter her room as she cleaned the chalkboard. His voice startled her.

"I went by the Country Swing and your apartment. You moved."

She continued cleaning the board after she turned to see him sitting at the back of the room.

"I never thought they'd approve it," he said.

"Shouldn't you be in the Bahamas?" she asked, still with her back to him.

"That can wait. I'm sorry—for everything."

She turned to him and walked slowly while she spoke. "J. D.'s sorry. Oh, that's a real comfort to us all."

She walked up to him with the chalk eraser clenched in one hand. "I want you to see something," she said.

He watched her leave her classroom. She stopped in the hallway then continued down the hall. He got up and followed her down the dark school hallway.

At the end of the hall, she unlocked a storage room door with a key and opened it, waiting for him to catch up. He stood in the doorway behind her when she flicked on the storage room lights. At the back of the room under a lone bulb was an ominous four and a half-foot copper statue of a little girl holding a kitten. It was made from hundreds of thousands of pennies. He followed her over to the sculpture.

"Missouri's school children gave their milk money to the Jerome survivors. An artist made this as a symbol of peace and healing after the disaster," she told him.

J. D. touched the girl's cheek, marveling at the likeness of a young girl. He turned to Ashlee. "I've seen this girl. In the disaster book. She was one of the children..."

"Marian Hunter. You met her the other day."

"That was her?"

"The sculptor modeled it from a photo of her taken just before the explosion."

"Why are you showing me this? Ya don't have to lay on the guilt, Ashlee. I feel plenty of guilt without this. But ya know what? If it wasn't me, someone else would sell that land. Maybe if I'd had security, I wouldn't have sold it, but I did. And I'm sorry for that more than anything. And that's something none of you will understand until you've been there. And I think you have some kind of connection to all this. What is that, Ashlee? Talk to me."

She paced the storage room, her steps loud and echoing as she thought about her words. "You can't live in this area and work in this town without feeling for these people. It's too late to reach you, J. D. It's done. I'm mad at you because you could have taken the survivors' money and let it be as they wanted. But you took the highest bidder without compassion."

"Ashlee, you don't know how I've suffered over this. Why do you think I'm still here? I haven't taken the money and run! I'm under some kind of pressure after selling that land to Stone. I don't know what it is but I have to find out."

"What are you looking for?" she asked impatiently.

"I don't know."

He hesitated before telling her more. "I found a key in my grandpa's house. A safe deposit key. I bought a list of Missouri banks because I can't find the bank where he kept the box. My big fear is I'm gonna have to get a list of banks in Iowa and Illinois too. It's drivin' me nuts."

"That's what you're doing in that treehouse?"

"Yeah."

"Why there?"

"I can't call from his house. I have these bad dreams, or, these real dreams all the time."

"So you think if you find that safe deposit box, you'll have your freedom from guilt?"

"Yeah, somethin' like that."

He went back over to the statue of the girl holding the kitten and faced it while speaking to Ashlee. "Ya know, it's so bizarre when I read about Kedloe's life in that book. I found myself interested in his twisted life. The way he killed his stepmom when he was a teenager by tampering with the stove. It blew up in her face. She died a terrible way. He got away with it, just like he got away with blowing up the school and killing and injuring all those people. You tell me all these things about these everyday people, the survivors, and what they went through and all. Well, it's just like today. People don't care about the victims. Not really. Oh, there are good people like you and Albert that go around picking up the pieces and holding things together, but it's the creeps like Kedloe and Stone that really get all the attention and interest about what they did. They seem to make history and we want to read all we can about them and the crazy things they did. You think we can ever learn anything good from Stone or Kedloe? It's just man's ability to hurt man, another way of doing it, for both of them."

When he turned to Ashlee, she was gone. There was no point in going after her. He was wrong and he knew it.

Albert promised he'd call, but he didn't want to. He knew if he telephoned old man Cochrand and told him the Kedloe place would be done in a week or so, it would only be trouble for quiet Jerome and the eldest survivor.

He made the call, but he didn't talk to Mr. Cochrand. Cochrand's nurse insisted on taking the message. She would pass it on to Mr. Cochrand, she told Albert, when he was more rested from his trip to Jerome.

When Albert hung up the phone after talking with

Cochrand's nurse, he was glad he didn't have to give a detailed progress report he promised Cochrand he'd give him. To tell the old man that rare black and white film footage of the disaster aftermath had been converted to videotape and would be sold by nearly every merchant in Jerome—might be a death blow.

Albert sat in his recliner puffing his unlit pipe, thinking, thinking of what his old friend Ray Dunn would say if he could see this Missouri Madness.

Albert thought this would be a good time to retire, to get away from all the little problems this thing would cause a cop. Chief Linn was officially retired anyway since he turned sixty-five. The township has paid him two hundred and twenty dollars a month for twelve years—just to drive around the county to see that all the doors and windows were locked that should be locked. He hadn't carried a gun since he turned sixty-five. And he hadn't prevented any crimes, because there weren't any. Until now. Albert removed his wire-rim glasses, puffed on his cherry wood pipe and twirled the gray hairs over his right eyebrow remembering the first time he really met Ray Dunn. It was May 18th, the day of the disaster.

The second explosion ripped shrapnel into his knee when Kedloe blew up himself and a few bystanders outside the damaged school. It was Ray who came over and helped young Albert Linn to his feet. Ray asked Albert where he lived. Albert pointed in the direction of his house, for he was too stunned to speak. He remembered gingerly walking home, all the while knowing that Ray had purposely come over to him and shielded him from seeing the horrible carnage from the second explosion.

Yes, Ray Dunn was a hero to Albert Linn; one of the main reasons he became a cop. And now this—a tourist attraction that was nothing but lunacy in a society gone mad, and a crime to anyone who was related to the Jerome School Disaster.

He had to think this out. If he got caught, Stone would come down hard and prosecute. The one responsible for all this would have to be out of the picture. He knew he would have to have help as he puffed faster and faster on his empty pipe while thinking of his timeframe. Was it worth going to prison for? he asked himself. The answer was as clear as that day in May over seven decades ago when innocent youth discovered that violence can strike out of the blue, teaching a tiny Missouri village that bad things can happen to good people, and that nothing as terrible could possibly ever happen to them again.

Stone's gold Cadillac was parked next to the exit side of his guardshack, facing the Dunn house. The Missouri Madness boss watched for an unmarked truck from St. Louis that was due to deliver what would most certainly be his attraction's most controversial piece.

Stone heard from his day guards that J. D. was on the phone all day across the road in a treehouse. From his Cadillac, he couldn't believe his eyes when he saw J. D. pacing a small circle while he talked into a headset mike. He noticed J. D. appeared to be angrily punching boards of the treehouse between calls.

Stone told his guard he would be right back and for the driver from St. Louis not to unload until he returned.

The King of Slugs could see Stone in his three-piece black business suit coming toward him. He took off his headset and sat on the floor of Oz, his legs dangling twelve feet off the ground as Ed Stone stood a few yards back looking up at J. D.

"I'd like to buy this place, J. D. I could use this ground for parking."

"I think I'd sell it to anyone but you, Stone."

"Why's that?" Stone smiled.

"I know I wouldn't have sold you that land if you'd told me what you were going to do with it." Stone smirked at J. D. while bobbing his head up and down.

"J. D., anybody who buys this place will sell to me eventually."

"Maybe."

"It's none of my business..but what in the hell are you doing up there?"

"You're right..it's none of your business. And I don't appreciate your crew workin' all night, makin' all that racket."

As Stone laughed, he saw the delivery truck he'd been waiting for. It turned off the main road and stopped in front of his guardshack.

"J. D., how would you like to be one of the first people to lay eyes on the star of Missouri Madness? Come on! It's free! It'll cost ya ten bucks later!"

J. D. stood by the back ramp of the truck as two sealed crates were carried into the Kedloe house by Stone's crew. The entire crew, some six dozen men, all stopped working, including the guard, to see who Stone billed as "the world's worst demon" on all his billboards. J. D. watched the men open the long crates. Inside the first crate was Mrs. Kedloe, a chalky-white mannequin wearing a black linen house dress with apron. The likeness from the photo in the disaster book was uncanny to J. D. As workers opened Kedloe's crate, J. D. asked Stone:

"There were no known photos of Kedloe. How'd you get..."

Stone removed a piece of paper from his breast pocket and gave it to J. D. "It's the only known image of him."

"Where'd you get this?"

"The Hannibal police had this sketch drawn."

J. D. could see the sinister face of an angry devil with his scowl and cruel lips, and those mean eyes. Then the Kedloe mannequin was revealed, matching the sketch J. D. held in his hands. Kedloe was just under six feet tall, dressed in forest green work pants with plaid shirt and black workshoes from the 1920s. The mannequin's hands were flexed open as if toying with something.

"Put him in his chair," Stone ordered the men. Stone placed a metal puzzle from his pocket into Kedloe's hands, a hobby of Kedloe's mentioned in the book.

"Where do you want her?" one of his crew asked.

"In the kitchen," Stone snapped, then he told his crew to get back to work, reminding them that opening day was June 1st.

J. D. looked around the Kedloe living room furnished in

austere rustic Americana from the early Twentieth Century.

The walls were covered with framed black and white disaster photos with inscriptions below them that J. D. recognized from the disaster book.

"I can't believe people will pay ten bucks to see a mannequin," J. D. said while reading one of the photos.

"I can't believe it either," Stone laughed.

On the late morning of May 27th, it began to drizzle. The Jerome Main Street's 1920-era light poles were being installed by Stone's contracting crew.

Ashlee had to park in the Middle School parking lot, for the Jerome downtown area around the Old School grounds was congested with media vehicles for Stone's press conference. J. D. arrived just then. He parked near Ashlee's car and tried to catch up with her before reaching the cluster of press and onlookers on the Old School grounds at the cupola, where Stone stood surrounded by his entourage.

The press conference began just when J. D. stood behind Ashlee and Albert. Albert was out of uniform. He noticed her holding Albert's hand as if needing support to get through this thing. Stone was smugly dressed in a business suit but wearing a yellow hard hat as if in command to answer any questions regarding the construction of Missouri Madness. At the back of the cupola behind Stone stood two Missouri Highway Patrolmen in uniform scanning the crowd for troublemakers. Stone smiled at the media.

"I guess we can begin now."

Television lights came on, lighting up the cupola this late gray morning as one reporter asked, "Mr. Stone, when will Missouri Madness be open for business?"

"My project manager informed me this morning that June 1st will be opening day, as long as the buses are delivered as promised."

"Mr. Stone, do you have any misgivings about your project?" another reporter asked.

"When you see hundreds of cars bumper-to-bumper in

Jerome, and twenty acres of parking ground filled..then ask me," Stone answered confidently.

Just then, a passerby in his vehicle yelled, "GO TO HELL, STONE!"

Stone appeared unruffled by the caustic remark, responding with, "Ya can't please everyone!" Stone laughed.

Another reporter asked, "Doesn't all this glorify Kedloe and what he did here?"

"That's subjective and will always be debated."

Albert barked above the reporters: "Stone, I've talked to survivors, and they don't want any money from this crazy scheme of yours!"

"Sir, I hear what you are saying. But there is one point you are forgetting—the last thing Kedloe would want is for anyone to profit from his deed. Back in 1927, after the disaster, there was no financial aid for victims in Jerome. It's late in coming, but I'm very proud to say, if Kedloe had a grave, he'd be turning in it every time a dollar was given to the very town he tried to destroy!"

Just then, Stone turned and unveiled the same bronze statue of the little girl holding the kitten that Ashlee had shown J. D.

"This statue was melted down from the pennies of Missouri children's milk money in 1927. I've made a deal with the Charter Township—they will display this symbol of healing on the Old School grounds and allow my tourists to walk these sacred grounds. And I will give one dollar to Ashlee Jessup and her survivors in need of care at Sunnyside Retirement Home!"

"WE DON'T WANT YOUR BLOOD MONEY, STONE!" Ashlee shouted above the applause.

"That not what the Township said!" Stone shot back.

"Can they do that?" Albert asked Ashlee. "I thought you owned this land."

"The Township is the trustee and maintains the property. We only can approve sale of the land."

"Now if you'll all move out to the Kedloe place, we can finish this interview!" Stone said, above the crowd.

As the crowd disbursed, Albert saw trouble walking toward them. It was Mr. Cochrand, escorted by his nurse. The old man made his way to the cupola. Albert limped over to the old man as Stone saw the survivor coming toward him and alerted the patrolmen. The patrolmen were poised to protect Stone from the 100-year-old survivor getting closer with the aid of his cane. Albert showed his police I. D. to the patrolmen and told them that the old man just wanted a few words with Stone; that he meant no harm and he was not armed. With guards on each side of him, Stone agreed to listen to the man as long as there were no reporters around.

His nurse stood a few steps behind him as Cochrand's tall, angular frame trembled on his cane when he handed Stone an old black and white photo of his young son with his palsied hand covered with liver spots and bulging blue veins. Cochrand's voice was deep and powerful as he spoke directly into Stone's eyes.

"That is my son, Bobby. I was at work ten miles away when I heard a muffled explosion coming from Jerome. I think I was one of the last parents to arrive at the school. The first thing I saw..was a row of little bodies covered with blankets. I walked right past them and started digging in the rubble. I was afraid to ask anyone if they'd seen Bobby. Then, I had to look under the blankets..thanking God each time it was not my boy. Going faster and faster from blanket to blanket..then..I found him. I remember being on my knees next to him, picking the plaster out of his mangled face. The only thing I could do was to get angry at God. So I beat the ground with my arms till they were bloody. To this day, Mr. Stone, I can't go to sleep covered with a blanket without seeing him there. There's not an hour in every day that I don't think about him. He was our only child. The grief killed my wife. See, Mr. Stone, you can't bring back that day and expect us to like it."

Cochrand took the photo from Stone's hand and walked away with his nurse and Albert helping him back to their rental car. Stone looked away from Ashlee's glare and smiled.

"Like I said: Ya can't please everybody."

Ashlee watched Stone escorted by the officers into a patrol car and driven away. She turned and saw J. D. standing on the grounds of the Old School. She went over to him. He had his hands in his pockets, his back to her. She noticed his eyes had been crying. He talked to her with his back to him, avoiding eye contact.

"Jesus, what have I done?" he groaned.

She rubbed the back of his neck tenderly with one hand then squeezed his shoulder with both hands as he continued.

"I've never had any kids. Maybe that's how I was able to sell the land. I read about Mr. Cochrand and the poor parents looking under the blankets for their children. I wasn't really moved until now. Seeing and listening to that old man made it so real."

J. D. pointed to where the sidewalk was in front of the school. "I read about the postal worker whose leg was blown off. He died in the arms of his wife..over there. Afterwards, they couldn't find Kedloe's body and must've wondered if he was still alive. Then they found his guts hanging from telephone lines. I keep seeing my grandpa working on these lines in these dreams I keep having."

She moved to face him. His head was bent down to his chest. She hugged him, wanted so much to help him, but couldn't; she knew she never could.

When they walked away from the school grounds to the Middle School parking lot, a stout, middle-aged man wearing dark sunglasses and a baseball cap stood reading the historical marker near the curb on Main Street. In the pelting drizzle under a gray sky, this stranger looked down Main at the crew installing gas lights. Then, he purposely walked over to the spot where the couple had stood just moments earlier. The stranger's hands were deep in his front jeans pockets below his navy blue windbreaker. He appeared to be getting a feel for the sacred ground where the Jerome School once stood. He was only doing what hundreds of visitors had done here since May 18th, 1927. He stood thinking about the discovery he made in the Hannibal Library today. He looked up the date May 18th in the annuls of history, a rather thick book that told what happened on each day of the year in history from January 1st to December 31st. Kedloe's deed wasn't mentioned in the book on May 18th, but the biggest explosion in modern history happened at exactly the same time of day on May 18th at Mt. Saint Helens, the biggest volcanic eruption in North America in recent history. He thought it was as if the devil himself claimed that day for hell to break loose.

Under his jacket, the stranger removed a copy of the same Jerome School Disaster book. In the book's index, he found the page that said Kedloe was born and raised in Tecumseh. He returned the book to a dry place under his jacket while walking back to his rental car.

Inside his rental car, he found the town Tecumseh on his Missouri map opened and flat on the car's front seat.

Ashlee drove past J. D.'s place, deciding not to follow him home. She looked across the road and saw the press converging into the Kedloe house, the home of the madman who had controlled her life since girlhood. She cruised along the county road at 55 and passed a finished billboard that advertised the crime of the Twentieth Century.

"Why don't I help him?" she asked herself, still feeling something for the man in the treehouse.

As she drove, she thought it odd that he never asked where she was living now. Then she thought of her senior year in Columbia, the year she decided to become a teacher and teach around the Hannibal area. Then she thought about her lovelife and how she had put it on hold. Springtime always made her think of that marriage thing that most women around here seem to fall into in their twenties. She resented her parents for not returning from Arizona and leaving her the family house to maintain in Thorpe. Why she moved back to there after J. D. sold that land, she wasn't real certain. Perhaps she wanted him to find her there and tell him everything she knew; then, take her to the Bahamas, where he would love her and be the love of her life.

But the twenty-three mile drive to Thorpe was proof enough to her that she could never let him into the legacy her family left her to guard. She checked her rear-view mirror often, making sure he wasn't following her. Again she had seen that hurt in his eyes when standing with him on the school grounds after Mr. Cochrand left. And she thought of how he was a victim too, over seventy years later; it was a fresh wound for him, and how he was suffering from his part in this madness that the others had learned to live with.

This was her home, she reminded herself, as she parked under the elms in the long driveway of the mauve-colored, three-story Victorian home in this town of 350 souls that she knew were going to bed every night with Missouri Madness in their prayers. They were unable to stop it..again.

Ashlee got out of her car and stood beside her open door breathing in spring's cool, floral air. She remembered when she was a girl of seven, her grandfather walking with her. He held her little hand so tightly in his while he explained his role on that terrible day in May. And years later, he talked about it one more time just weeks before he died.

She was fifteen then. From then on she always knew she would always protect him and make her family proud of the way she lived.

She started to cry, too enervated to close her car door with authority. She wanted to help the King of Slugs with his guilt, for guilt is a terrible thing she knew too well. She knew it could kill him and destroy any hope of ever having a life of inner peace, something she knew Ray Dunn's grandson deserved. Besides, she loved him.

The Stretch

At two in the morning, his hotel room's phone rang only once. He was ready for his wake-up call. Mr. Cochrand was not asleep; he hung up the phone after lifting it off its cradle. He had been lying on top of the bedcovers fully dressed with the volume muted on the weather channel as his dentures soaked on the bathroom counter and his nurse slept in the adjoining room.

He reached for his cane and felt the old aches and pains in his joints he used to feel before moving to Florida. When he got to his feet with the aid of his cane, he knew he'd have to conserve his energy to make it all the way home on his flight from St. Louis at eleven this morning. His bag was already packed and standing in front of the door. After putting in his dentures, he looked at his wrist watch. From his billfold he removed the same photo of his son and put it in his shirt pocket near his heart.

Yes, this would be a stretch for a man about to reach the century mark on this planet.

When Cochrand drove up to a gas pump in his rental car at a convenience store, he had to take his medication for his heart just to get out of the car, for he would tire easily behind the wheel. He got out with the aid of his cane and opened the trunk to remove the three gallon gas cans he bought in a hardware store that day while his nurses were getting ready for breakfast. The old man started to fill one of the cans with gas from the pump after waving to the clerk for him to turn on his pump.

When he left the convenience store parking area, he saw one of the Missouri Madness billboards on the main highway recently finished. The billboard is a montage of the Old Jerome School; Kedloe's farm; a 1920-era truck parked on the refurbished Jerome Main Street with a directional pointing arrow and the words "3 miles to Jerome, Missouri. Home of America's most despicable crime and the world's worst demon. The Tour Of Your Life. Opens June 1st."

At 3:15, Sunnyside was dark except for the light on at the

nurses' station. Outside one of the room's windows, Cochrand poked the ground in the dark with his cane until he found what he was looking for and stuffed it inside his jacket pocket. Then, he painfully walked with his cane toward the idling rental car.

At 3:30, Cochrand parked in the old country cemetery seven miles south of Jerome, a place where his wife and son were buried. His wife had died in Florida, but wanted to lie beside her only child and her parents. Cochrand knelt at his wife's grave and put the photo of his son against the flat marble marker. He rubbed the marble with his palsied hand and whispered that he would take care of everything.

Cochrand's hands were gripped tightly at the top of the steering wheel as he closed in on Missouri Madness. Just then, he heard old sounds from that day in May—the approaching siren of a fire engine; the chaotic scramble and digging of rescue workers in the rubble; the screams and moans of parents and injured children. The old man's strong hands got tighter and tighter around the steering wheel as he closed in on the Kedloe place. Then, in the middle of his lane, he saw a vision of the young girl holding the kitten, alive and not a statue. He swerved to avoid hitting her and overturned in the ditch, his car soon in flames.

The explosion woke J. D. from a dead sleep. He hurried to the front room window and could see flames a quarter mile away down the road in front of his house. Quickly, he dialed 911 and told them there was a fire and to hurry.

Cochrand was barely conscious on the front seat of his rental when he took the handgun from his pocket and fired one round into his temple rather than burn alive.

By the time J. D. arrived, the car was completely engulfed in flames. The Jerome fire engine was on its way, its siren getting closer.

At dawn, the ambulance drove away with Cochrand's body as Albert and J. D. watched the tow truck haul away the rental car. Just then, Stone drove up in his Cadillac.

"What happened?" Stone asked.

"The old man who reamed you out yesterday. He's dead. He had three full gas cans in his trunk, and I don't think he wanted anyone to see your opening day," Albert said.

"Too bad," Stone said, then drove away thinking about the publicity this would give his attraction. He thought that bad publicity would be good for him and called the Hannibal newspaper from his car phone.

Later that morning, Ashlee got no answer after she knocked on J. D.'s front door. She walked around to the back of the house and looked up to the treehouse and could see J. D.'s leg sticking out from under the closed shower curtain. She climbed to the treehouse platform after she called out to him and got no response. She found J. D. asleep on the floor and tossing from a bad dream.

She woke him and stopped him from falling out of the treehouse. "What are you doing up here?" she asked.

"Mr. Cochrand was killed...He was on his way..."

"I know. Albert called me this morning. Can you make it down?"

"Yeah."

Ashlee led the way slowly down each step to the base of Oz.

A little later, J. D. is under the covers on his grandpa's bed when Ashlee brought him a cup of tea. He was burnt-out calling banks. She sat on the side of his bed while he sipped tea with his head propped by two pillows.

"I heard Cochrand's car explode and when I got there, I saw him burning. I've never seen anything like it. It was horrible," he said, still numb from the sight. "I want to run away from all of this. But I can't."

As he drove to the Tecumseh County Courthouse, he thought Tecumseh was one of the most charming towns he'd ever seen in America. The trees were verdant and tall and lined with such precision. They shaded magnificent Victorian homes that were meticulously maintained with care, and each one distinctly different in design and color. He thought it odd that on such a beautiful spring day, not many of the town's inhabitants were out walking in the sunshine.

He parked his rental car on the town square and marveled at the retail shops on all four blocks that squared around the stately courthouse made of red brick. Again, not many people about and there were many open parking spaces in downtown Tecumseh.

He kept on his dark sunglasses when he entered the county archives area in the County Clerk's office. He hoped the middle-aged clerk who approached him did not recognize him. She didn't. The stranger's voice had a distinct, soft, British accent when he smiled and introduced himself as Darin Pell, a fictitious name he thought of on the spur of the moment.

He spent an hour in the courthouse with the friendly woman. As he strolled leisurely along the clean cement sidewalk in front of the courthouse on his way to find a restaurant to grab a bite, he remembered the way the clerk's eyes widened when he introduced himself and said:

"I'm looking for any living descendants of an Andrew Kedloe. I thought perhaps you could help me locate any of his surviving relatives."

She allowed him to pour over birth and death records. He was able to see that a pattern was forming that he kept hidden from the clerk. When he found out all that he could, he asked for directions to the Catholic Cemetery and thanked her; but then, she told him something that everyone in Tecumseh knew—she said she was a friend of the neighbor to Kedloe when he was a teenager. She told him Kedloe killed his stepmother by rigging the stove to blow up in her face. The neighbor thought it strange how Kedloe was not the least bit upset or breathing hard when he came to her door to get help for his dying stepmother. The clerk went on and on about "How can a boy do such a terrible thing?"

As he ate his meal in the Tecumseh Café, he was thinking of something he was told by an American writer years ago. "The difference between Brits and Yanks when it comes to crime is that Americans want to know all the details why it happened, while the English go about the business of finding out what happened."

He knew this was an American crime. By far the most cowardly deed ever committed on any land. And he knew he had to reverse or suspend his inherent ability to get to the bottom of the thing. Mr. Pell knew that he too must know why as the Americans, not why Kedloe did such a thing—why tell them now.

For three hours he walked the Tecumseh Catholic Cemetery meticulously looking for names on his list that might be on graves in this massive place.

Late in the afternoon, Pell rang a doorbell at a modest home he'd found listed in the phone book. He removed his sunglasses as the front door opened and again hoped he would not be recognized. An elderly woman with poor eyesight and good hearing allowed him to enter her home when she heard him mention the Jerome School Disaster.

It was dark when he left the woman's house. His trained memory was swimming in photos and bits of information the woman gladly shared with the stranger. It would all be sorted out soon and his decision made.

That evening, in the Sunnyside dining room, Ashlee sat next to Albert listening to the survivors. They were all confused about the opening of Missouri Madness and animated about Cochrand's death.

"Can't something be done to stop this?" one of the survivors said, looking at Albert.

Albert answered with the fact that Stone had 24-hour security at the place.

"Still, something ought to be done," another survivor said.

At that moment, a nurse came into the room and whispered something to Ashlee. Ashlee left the room with the nurse; she feigned a calm demeanor, not wanting to alarm the survivors.

"Did she say anything?" Ashlee asked while walking briskly with the nurse to and into a room at the end of the hallway.

The nurse told Ashlee she couldn't make it out as they entered the room.

There on her bed in her private room was Marian Hunter,

the survivor who lost her leg in the disaster and recently moved in to Sunnyside. Her vitals were read on a screen by Ashlee and the nurse.

"I better call an ambulance," the nurse said, leaving Ashlee alone with the woman.

Ashlee leaned down close to Marian's face while holding her hand. "Marian, it's Ashlee. Is there anything you want to say, Marian?"

The old woman mumbled something incoherent, then died. The machine monitoring her heart stopped.

In the hallway, Ashlee told the same nurse and Albert, "She's gone. Do you know if she heard anything about what happened to Mr. Cochrand?"

"I don't believe anyone's been in her room," the nurse said.

Just after the ambulance quietly drove away with Marian's body, Ashlee and Albert stood near their vehicles in the Sunnyside parking lot looking at the new, nostalgic Main Street lights flickering on.

"Those lights sure bring back the memories," Albert reflected.

"Good ones?" Ashlee asked.

"Oh, yes. I was thinking how I used to ride my sled so fast down Main, passing my friends, laughing. And we'd walk back up the hill and do it again and again. Marian's father owned the feed store. Her mother would bring us hot chocolate. Her house was just over there," he pointed. "They were nice people."

"Did you know her well?" Ashlee asked.

"Not well. I don't remember seeing her much after the disaster. She moved to Hannibal."

"I heard some of the residents at Sunnyside lived here because Ray Dunn helped pay for their care."

"That's right," Albert said.

"Why'd they tear down that Old School?"

"Memories, I s'pose. Nobody really talked about it."

Just then, J. D. pulled up in his car and parked next to

them. Ashlee and Albert walked over to J. D., who stayed behind the wheel.

"You get some rest?" Ashlee asked.

"Not really," J. D. answered, pinching his tired eyes.

"We lost another one," Albert told him.

"Who?"

"Marian Hunter. You met her at her house on my route," Ashlee said.

An awkward pause until Albert said coldly to J. D. "I thought you'd be gone by now."

"I want to sell the house, finish a few things."

"Well, I'll be on my way," Albert said before he hugged Ashlee goodbye.

They watched Albert drive off in his patrol car.

"Where are you living now?" he asked her.

"In my parents' house."

"Where's that?"

"In Thorpe."

"Thorpe? Where's that?"

"North of here."

Even though she sounded distant and cold toward him: "Can I call you?"

She wrote her phone number on a piece of paper and handed it to him.

"Look, I want to thank you for coming over today. The tea was good. I know this thing I did is still between us. I'm sorry."

"You've said that."

"I know. I just want you to know I wish we'd met under different circumstances."

"Me, too," she courtesy-smiled. "Are you going to keep looking for that bank?"

"Yeah."

"What if you don't find it?"

"I want to see what it's like here when Stone's place opens."

She watched him drive away. She knew she had given him a wrong number. If he comes to Thorpe, he does, she told herself.

When J. D. returned home, he was tired. He could see the security guard sitting in front of a glass window inside the lighted guardshack. He could see that the moon was full above the treehouse and had a vanilla-crème/orange glow. When he reached his front door, a car drove onto his lot and parked next to his car. The stranger in the rental car was told about this man who sold the Kedloe land to Stone.

"Excuse me, sir, but are you Mr. Dunn?"

J. D. is apprehensive. "Who are you?"

"My name is Darin Pell. I'm a journalist from England. I wanted to ask you a few questions about that place across the road."

"What's England care about that place for?"

The man stepped closer to J. D. "I heard you sold the land to the developer."

"I don't want to talk about it," J. D. said.

"I really could use your help, Mr. Dunn. I was in Tecumseh today and had a nice chat with a relative of Mr. Kedloe."

"Come in," Jack said with his back to the stranger.

They sat in the front room; both men appeared stiff and awkward.

"What about Tecumseh?" J. D. asked the stranger.

"I was talking to a woman who is a niece of Kedloe's, his sister's daughter. She told me your grandfather bought Kedloe's land from Mrs. Kedloe's family about twenty years after the disaster. I thought your grandfather might have talked to you about why he bought the land."

"He never said anything to me."

"It seems most of Kedloe's relatives moved out of the area and even changed their names after his terrible deed."

"Can you blame them?"

"I suppose not."

"How does all this affect my life?" J. D. asked cynically.

"I don't know. I suppose I'm trying to get a feel for this Missouri Madness for my report."

"Did you hear about Mr. Cochrand?" J. D. asked.

"The man from Florida killed in the auto accident, yes, a terrible thing."

"Cochrand changed the way I feel."

"How's that?" the stranger inquired softly.

"I don't know exactly. It's overwhelming sometimes. A couple things are keeping me here and won't let me leave."

"A couple things?"

"A key I found that fits a safe deposit box. I'm looking for that box. It was my grandfather's."

"What do you think you'll find?"

"I don't know."

"What was the other thing?"

"A woman."

"Ah, yes, and you've fallen in love with the woman?" the stranger smiled.

"Love, what is love, Mr…"

"Pell. I can't say what love is for you. For me, it's truth, a wondrous true feeling of wanting to be with somebody."

"Do you think I made a mistake by selling that land, Mr. Pell?"

"That's something left to a higher power than I, Mr. Dunn. Time will tell what's right or wrong," the man smiled.

J. D. stopped himself from telling this man about the letter and the teacher his grandfather loved in his dreams he was having.

"Right. Time will tell," J. D. agreed.

Mr. Pell stood up. "Well, I don't mean to impose. I guess I'll be on my way. Good luck to you, Mr. Dunn."

J. D. accepted his handshake.

He watched Pell drive away from his property. He felt like he'd seen him somewhere before.

Opening day, June 1st. J. D. started calling banks earlier than usual from Oz. He wanted to see the first customers of Missouri Madness. At first, nothing. Then, Stone showed up riding in the late 1920-era bus of the five buses that would shuttle his tourists to the Old School grounds and back. The drivers, all women, had been trained in St. Louis, getting familiar with the tight clutch and rough gear shifter, along with getting familiar with the disaster and the strange turning axis.

Stone only hired women to drive his expensive school buses that J. D. thought looked like street cars he had ridden at Disneyland. Each driver would be the tour guide for groups no larger than fifty with twenty-five at a time walking through the Kedloe house before being herded into the Kedloe barn, where a surprise awaited them before a maximum of fifty tourists were shuttled along the same route Kedloe took to the Old School.

A large television monitor inside each bus showed the black and white videotape after the disaster as the driver talked into her headset. The buses would then park in front of the Old School grounds. After they read the historical marker, each driver would escort her group over to the actual school grounds where Kedloe's second attack was explained. After that, the tourists were given a forty-minute break to roam around the area taking pictures, have a bite in the Jerome Café, and hopefully buy souvenirs from the anxious Jerome storekeepers who invested heavily in Stone's venture.

J. D. could see that Stone's opening day was going to please the Hannibal casino operator. As the King of Slugs kept pounding his list, eliminating bank after bank, he could see bus after bus leave with another full load of tourists every fifteen minutes non-stop until seven in the evening.

As he watched from his grandfather's chair in the front room, the last bus returning with tourists, he had this urge to talk to Ashlee. He went to the bedroom and dialed the number she gave him. As he returned to the front room, knowing she gave him a wrong number, it dawned on him that the stranger, Mr. Pell, resembled the mannequin of Kedloe that Stone had shown him in the Kedloe house. That's where he had seen him before, he told himself. Could that man have been Kedloe's son or some relative? he wondered. Why else would he have gotten people there to talk to him in Tecumseh? he thought. Maybe he really was a journalist from England, he told himself as he went into the bathroom to take a shower in order to wash the day of rejection away.

Later that night, J. D. drove around Hannibal looking for the stranger's rental car in the nicer hotels and motels.

No luck finding Mr. Pell. Maybe he left town, he said to himself. As he closed in on his house, he could hear the faint sound of a fire engine. Just then, at the same spot where Mr. Cochrand swerved into the ditch, J. D. saw a raging fire—his grandfather's house was on fire. After he parked on the road in front of his house, he couldn't believe what he saw. Oz had crashed through the roof of the house and was in flames. He thought of the key and ran for the front door. He kicked open the front door and saw that the front room was in flames, shielding his face from the heat with his forearm. The treehouse was shattered to pieces about the front room. He picked up pages from his bank list and stuffed them under his shirt while he made his way through the burning limbs of Oz toward the crucifix still hanging on the wall. As he reached for the cross, a burning limb crashed onto his shoulder, knocking him to the floor.

Outside the house, firemen arrived and heard J. D. scream. They rushed inside and soon carried J. D.'s smoldering body out the front door and placed him gently on the ground near his "For Sale" sign. He was coughing from smoke inhalation. A fireman told another fireman to get an ambulance dispatched and to notify the burn unit as he removed J. D.'s smoldering shirt and found pages of his bank list and his Bahamas poster. Next, the fireman gently opened one of J. D.'s clenched hands.

The fireman is stunned. "Jesus."

The safe deposit box key number 78 is branded into J. D.'s palm.

That night, J. D. was in a Hannibal hospital bed with heavy bandages covering both his hands up to his forearms. He had minor burns on his face and neck and most of his hair was burned off, including his eyebrows. A nurse entered his room to check on him. He opened his eyes and saw his charred Bahamas poster hanging on the wall.

"Key," he mumbled to the nurse.

The nurse leaned down in order to hear her patient. "The key," he repeated.

"The key?"

J. D. nodded yes.

"Oh, yes!" The nurse opened the drawer of his bedside table and showed him his precious key. "It's safe and sound in the drawer, okay?"

He smiled at her, then she put the key back into the drawer.

"Must be an important key to wear it in your hand." She gave her patient a drink of water from a flex straw, then told him to get some rest. She left the room smiling and shaking her head at the poster.

He closed his swollen eyes and could feel the burns on his wrapped stomach every breath he took. He knew he was lucky to be alive; he blocked out thinking about who could have set fire to his grandpa's little house by thinking about his dream girl. But that only led him to think about Ashlee. Maybe she'll visit me tomorrow, he hoped. She's got to hear about this from Albert. He fell asleep fast from the sedative he had been given earlier.

Chief Linn shined his flashlight on the base of Oz and rubbed his free hand over the smooth surface made by the blade of a chain saw. He had already talked to the guard on duty across the road, and of course Stone's man saw nothing and heard nothing. It had to be Stone who did this, he knew. And only someone on Stone's payroll who knew this was coming, would play dumb to not hearing a chain saw at night out here in the sticks.

At first, Ray Dunn's best friend was relieved to hear that his grandson was not in critical condition with his burns; but, Albert did mutter to himself that the son-of-a-bitch got what he deserved for startin' this whole gawd-damn mess.

The old cop knew it was time to retire full-time soon as he looked across the road at the dark outline of the Kedloe house. He could hardly believe it was really there. He blinked at a memory he hadn't consciously thought of since that night.

It was the first Halloween after the disaster. He was trick-or-treating with a few of his classmates when they knocked on George Hammon's door. Little George was the most scarred of the survivors; he remembered the fear he saw in the boy's eyes when he opened his door. And now, for the first time in over seventy years, he realized it was not George's fear, it was mine, he said to himself. That terribly scarred little boy had seen all the fear and pain from that day in May reflected in my eyes.

If anyone knew about fear, Albert Linn sure did. And he knew that place across the road was built and supported by that same fear he had helped promote for so many years.

"The Lord doesn't send the law," he snorted to himself, that old proverb Ray used to tell him in jest.

Ray used to talk about how insurance companies, the media, and especially the police—all exploited fear wholesale to the public. A public he knew too well that was only one paycheck away from anarchy and violent chaos.

"So why shouldn't that place prosper?" he asked the darkness. It feeds every nerve of fear they've been programmed to feel. Kedloe will keep them insured; he will give them all the worst possible news to think about; and they will all spend more money on their security for their homes, schools, and their streets.

Yes, Albert Henry Linn would announce his retirement. And no one would care. Another would take his place and make his rounds, another would put on this uniform and play the game of false sense of security. For ever since that day when Kedloe ambushed and murdered his town—he knew that bad things can happen to good people without warning, and that there is no security between the cradle and the grave.

Like Ray Dunn, he had lived his life to protect his town from being hurt by monsters like Kedloe. And now Ed Stone was hurting his town and making money from it. Something had to be done about that, he knew. Just like he knew the light of morning would reveal nothing he needed to know about this arson. Stone had acted like Kedloe—swift and powerful without warning after careful planning.

Now as he focussed across the road, he could see the media

vehicles stacking up at the guardshack to promote the success of that terrible deed. Stone only needed one good day and he acted. Albert knew Stone wanted the Dunn property for parking, and he wanted J. D. gone.

By late morning, J. D. had been lying awake watching the rain fall under the gray sky for two hours from his hospital bed. No breakfast. No Ashlee. Maybe later, he told himself, with his head turned away from the door and hoping for her to enter.

His nurse came in and inspected his wrappings. He thought she was toying with his spirits when she spoke.

"You have a visitor."

He perked up instantly, thinking it was Ashlee.

"A Mrs. Bordon," she continued.

"Who?"

"She's a ninety-year-old retired nurse from this hospital. She was at the Jerome School Disaster."

"Oh, Jesus..I don't want to see..."

"She was a friend of your grandfather's."

Her patient's deep breath told her to say: "I'll bring her in."

"On one condition," he said as the nurse walked away. "You come and take her out of here in ten minutes."

She agreed, then left the room, soon returning with the elderly Mrs. Bordon. She escorted the old lady up to her patient's bed, where she held onto the bed's railing. Just before the nurse left them alone, J. D. called out to his nurse.

"See ya in ten."

J. D. and Mrs. Bordon exchanged awkward smiles. "So, I s'pose you want to know why I sold the land, " he told her.

"What's that?" she smiled, turning her good ear to the man.

"Never mind," he said with a courtesy-smile. Then, she started to speak as if this was very important for her to be telling him this now.

"I was on duty here when they brought the kids in. When I

heard Ray's house was burned down, I first thought that one of those kids in the Jerome Disaster may have done it. If so, I know they didn't mean to hurt you. I saw how they suffered and braved through their ordeal. It was horrible."

J. D. nodded with understanding, then winced from his own pain when he shifted his body a bit.

"It was terrible in many ways long after. Oh how those families struggled to pay for care, and some couldn't get insurance or get a good job. A lot of good people helped them in many ways. I know the banker, Mr. Jessup, felt responsible. He was a fine man."

"Did you say Jessup?"

"Yes, Bernard Jessup's bank in Thorpe was about to foreclose on Kedloe's place just before he blew up the school. I know Mr. Jessup helped a bunch of those kids pay their medical bills."

J. D. was excited. His eyes moved back and forth as if playing a pinball machine. He raised each bandaged hand separately to see if he could move his fingers as the old nurse rambled on about poor Mr. Jessup. Just then, as his nurse entered his room to get Mrs. Bordon after ten minutes as agreed, J. D. snapped at his nurse.

"Would you please give us a few more minutes?"

In a slow and deliberate manner, J. D. asked his elderly visitor what the name of Jessup's bank was.

"The Bank of Thorpe," she replied.

"There's no bank in Thorpe."

"It's been closed for years. Soon after Mr. Jessup died, they closed it."

"Who closed it?"

"His son."

"Does his son still live in the area?"

"He retired to Arizona."

J. D. thought fast while looking at Mrs. Bordon.

Ashlee sat in the patrol car with Albert, parked on Ray's

land, facing the black rubble of Oz and Ray Dunn's house. The rain had put an end to any smoldering. They had been sitting here for ten minutes without saying a word. He had told her that J. D. was listed in satisfactory condition with burns on his hands. She thought that Albert did this, until he broke their silence as the traffic at Missouri Madness was much heavier than opening day.

"I guess Stone can get all the parking he wants now."

"Are you saying he did this?"

"As sure as I know I didn't do it."

All afternoon J. D. was alone in his private room, his head turned to the window that looked out to a Hannibal residential street. A thousand times he thought of the banks he called from Oz while she knew all along he was wasting his time.

A night-shift nurse came into his room while J. D. was presumed asleep. She clicked off his nightlight above his head then exited his room. He opened his eyes, kicked off his covers, and in his hospital gown he managed to painfully get to his knees on his bed, whereupon he flipped on his nightlight with his nose. He gingerly scooted down to the foot of his bed and got to his feet on the floor, and slowly he made his way toward his bedside table. No way could he use his bandaged hands to open the table's drawer so he laid on his back on the floor and used his bare feet to open the drawer. He painfully stood, then he bent down into the drawer and pulled out a set of pajamas with his teeth, placing them on the bed.

Next, J. D. got onto his back on the bed and winced from pain while using his feet and legs to worm his pajama bottoms up his lower body until he stopped because he felt a bowel movement coming on.

"Oh God, not now," he grumbled.

He wiggled off his pajama bottoms, then swiveled around with his head at the foot of the bed and pushed both pajama top and bottom under the pillow with his feet. Then he flipped off the nightlight with his nose, swiveled around with his head on the pillow and pushed his service light with his elbow just before getting to his knees and using his teeth to cover himself with his covers.

He tried to conceal his fatigue when the nightshift nurse came into his room to answer his call.

"I have to go to the bathroom," he said humbly. The nurse placed a bedpan under him and exited the room.

A little bit later, the nurse covered J. D. with covers after removing the bedpan. "Thank you," he smiled.

As she stretched to turn off the light above his head, he asked her if she'd do him a small favor. "There's a key in that drawer. It's sort of a good luck charm. Could you please put the key on top of the table so I can see it? Oh, and could you please leave the light on?"

Later, J. D. was wearing his hospital gown over pajama bottoms and slippers while he used his teeth to pick up his folded cash inside the drawer. With difficulty he rolled the cash into a wad with his tongue and positioned the money inside his mouth against his puffy cheek. Next, he saw a wrapped toothbrush on the table that he picked up with his lips and positioned the bristle end of the toothbrush into the other side of his mouth, leaving the handle of the toothbrush sticking out. Next, he scooped up the safe deposit box key with his lips and placed it inside his mouth against his lower lip.

He took a deep breath, walked over to the door, got on his back, twisted open the door's handle with his slippered feet, jerked open the door in grimacing pain, just enough space to wedge one foot behind the door to keep it from closing. Lowering his foot, he managed to stand while keeping his foot wedged behind the door. He caught his breath and peeked out into the empty hallway.

J. D. hobbled out of his room and slipped down the hallway without being noticed. He thought of his dream girl that he left behind as he kept hearing the Love and Rockets song "So Alive" playing in his head all the way downstairs, those painful stairs that led him outside to the hospital's main entrance unnoticed. He kept hearing the music in his head as he limped away from the hospital.

It was getting late. It was the kind of summer night when the wind blew easy and convinced a tired mind he'd led a life unlived. He'd been sitting in his patrol car, parked alongside the Old School grounds, not far from the historical marker. He'd been thinking about putting a bullet in Stone's head. So far, he would be in uniform when he did it; he'd have Stone meet him alone at some isolated spot to talk about his security problems at Missouri Madness.

But it was Albert who was being watched now. The glow/orange of his cigarette sucked bright in front of his face from behind the wheel of his rental car parked two hundred yards away in the Middle School parking lot.

"So Alive" faded out of J. D.'s head as he waited in line in a convenience store. Some young men buying beer were cracking up between themselves over the strange man's appearance behind them—clad in a green hospital gown with baggy pajama bottoms, slippers, drool and liquid/clear snot dripped from his chin and upper lip. His hair is burnt down to a mohawk butch, not to mention the protruding toothbrush handle, swollen cheek and lower lip.

They paid for their beer and left the store while laughing hard at J. D., who stepped up to the counter of the alarmed convenience store clerk.

"You need help?" the male clerk asked.

"Please call me a cab," J. D's said, his words garbled.

"What?" the clerk asked.

More slobbering garble. "A cab! Taxi!" J. D. drooled.

The clerk had no idea what J. D. was saying until J. D. used his bandaged hands to mimic driving a car and hitting the horn, garbling louder. "Honk! Honk! A cab!"

"A cab! Sure! I'll call ya a cab, buddy!" The clerk found a phone number, picked up the phone and dialed the number as J. D. smiled with slobber hanging in ever-lengthening drips from his toothbrush as:

This stranger from England, the journalist Pell, dropped his cigarette discreetly out his window, not sure if it would be considered littering. He mainly did not want to appear overtly callous and perhaps get on the wrong side of the law.

He knew the policeman was a Jerome School Disaster survivor and that he was a close friend of Mr. Ray Dunn. He looked at his list under his dome light and saw that Albert Linn was still on it.

Albert saw the man get out of his car and begin to head his way from the other side of the Old School grounds. He thought the man walked as if the Old School was still there, staying on an invisible path of the very sidewalk that once bordered the south side of the main school building. This made Albert's heart start to beat faster as if it intuitively sensed danger was approaching from the licorice-black darkness. Besides, there was some strange thing that was familiar about this man. Did he know him? he wondered. The closer the man got to him—the more he thought he knew him from somewhere, but in the June night with no moon, he could not make out his face.

He watched the stranger's empty hands, making sure there was no weapon. Chief Linn's window was rolled down; he was purposely unarmed now, so he'd be unable to act out on his thoughts of killing Stone. Then, as the man came within twenty yards of the patrol car's front bumper, Albert's heart felt as it it was going to explode—faster and faster it beat until the stranger's face was at his window and the old cop's face twisted and writhed with a shock that was too much for his ticker.

"Excuse me, sir, I wonder if you can help me." The man had no idea that Albert was having a full-blown heart attack, all because this man was a dead-ringer for Kedloe. Albert slumped forward grabbing his chest, face-down onto his steering wheel.

The stranger looked down the empty Main Street for any sign of help. "Sir, are you ill?"

"My heart," Albert groaned.

A yellow cab pulled up and parked in front of the Hannibal

convenience store and left the engine running. J. D. came out from
hiding near the side of the store. He limped toward the rolled-
down window of the young black cab driver. The wide-eyed cab
driver was alarmed, for his fare looked like an escapee from the
hospital with slobber dripping from his mouth and toothbrush.

"You call a cab?"

J. D. nodded yes then walked stiff-legged over to the cab's
front passenger door. With his mouth agape, the cab driver can see
J. D.'s toothbrush-drooling/puffy face gesturing with his raised
bandaged hands that he was unable to open the passenger door.
The driver hesitated, then reluctantly leaned over and opened his
front passenger door. He watched his fare get on his front seat
slowly and in obvious pain before he closed the door with the
inside of his raised forearm at the top of the door.

"To the hospital?" he hoped.

J. D. fervently grunted while he shook his head no and said
with slobbering garble: "Thorpe."

"Where?"

More garble. "Thorpe!"

After he watched spittle drop onto his clean black leather
seat, he asked "The shelter?"

His passenger is frustrated, grunting and shaking his head
no. J. D. took a deep breath through his nose then raised his
bandaged right hand with his palm facing the driver; he tried to let
the driver know that his hand was in Missouri.

"Hand? Hannibal!" the driver yelled excitedly.

J. D. opened the glovebox and took out a Missouri map by
raking it out. The driver took the map and opened it under the
dome light. J. D. leaned down and pointed at a spot on the map
with the end of his slippery toothbrush. The driver squinted at the
spot on the map.

"Thorpe?" he said.

"Thorpe!" J. D. smiled while nodding yes.

"Thorpe is a thirty-dollar fare from here, man. You got
that much cash on ya?"

J. D. nodded yes and tilted his head back with his mouth
open wide, revealing his cash.

"You got your money in your mouth?"

He nodded yes with a slobbering smile.

"You ready to travel, ain't ya?" he said as he drove the cab away from the convenience store.

Mr. Pell was driving Albert's patrol car ninety miles per hour, headed for Hannibal, not knowing where to find a hospital. He kept glancing over at the old cop's chest that was leaned over to the right, his head on his passenger door armrest.

The stranger's mind was on the old lady in Tecumseh who was related to Kedloe. She had mentioned to him that he looked like Kedloe; she even showed him the only known photo of the madman in middle age, and he was astonished at the resemblance. Now he knew why he was here. The man who chose him was from Hannibal and must have seen the same photo.

"Poor guy," he mumbled, referring to Albert, for he had purposely stayed away from any of the Jerome survivors who may have seen or known the man who tried to murder them. He thought the policeman, Mr. Linn, would not be affected this way. He was wrong.

The Hannibal city limits were closing in. He could take the first exit and ask the first person he saw where the nearest hospital was. At a red light, Pell ran it and pulled right in front of the cab J. D. was riding in. Albert's patrol car blocked its way when the light turned green. The confused cab driver thought about jumping out of his cab and letting the cops arrest his drooling passenger, an obvious hospital escapee.

J. D. could plainly see it was Geronimo's car. He turned his head away thinking it was Albert, but then he heard that distinct British accent of the journalist ask his driver where the nearest hospital was located. J. D.'s quick side-glance revealed Pell's face to him when he sped off in Albert's patrol car. What was Pell doing driving Albert's car to the hospital? he wondered.

The cab drove slowly along Thorpe's small business district that was a bit bigger than Jerome. J. D. leaned forward

with his dripping toothbrush handle still in his mouth. He then
saw an abandoned bank building. He motioned for the driver to
park while he pointed excitedly at the old building. The driver
parked and looked down at his meter that read $29.10. He pointed
at the fare total and smiled at J. D.

"I guess it's time to cough it up."

The driver scooted closer to J. D. after turning on his dome
light. He watched J. D. remove his toothbrush and hold onto it
between his bandages before he tilted his head back. The driver
did not want to reach inside J. D.'s mouth for his fare.

"How 'bout I use that toothbrush?"

J. D. nodded yes. The driver talked as he worked the brush
end inside J. D.'s mouth, trying to get J. D.'s wet cash out.
"Wider. That's it. I do need this job. I can't eat this fare."

He scraped the slimy cash out of J. D.'s mouth and saw it
drop onto his seat. He got a hanky from his shirt pocket and used
the toothbrush and the hanky to unwad the roll of wet cash as J. D.
moved around his tired jaw. Now he could finally speak with
only the key behind his lower lip.

"These are all hundreds," the driver said, after inspecting J.
D.'s stash.

"Take one and keep the change," J. D. said. "I'll give ya
another hundred if ya give me your shirt and throw in that hanky.
And I'll need your help to put on the shirt."

The driver quickly peeled off his shirt and helped J. D. put
it on.

"After ya get yer other hundred, put the rest of my cash in
the shirt pocket, please."

"Sure thing, man. Anything else?"

"It would be good if you could wipe off my face a bit."

The driver wiped J. D.'s face dry with the hanky and went
to put the hanky in the same pocket with the money.

"Other pocket, please," J. D. smiled.

Then the driver started to return the toothbrush into J. D.'s
mouth, but J. D. turned his head to the side. "I need one more
small favor before that goes back in."

"Sure, man."

"I need two quarters, one under my tongue, the other one between my lips, then the toothbrush in the corner of my mouth."

He watched the cab drive away in the deserted main drag of tiny Thorpe. There wasn't another soul around. He crossed the street and stood in front of the old bank building, just looking at it. This was the prize he'd tried so hard to find on the phone. This was the place that could give him a life for the first time in his wandering life of a nomad, an American gypsy. This place could free him to move on. What if it didn't? he thought, as he looked down both sides of the street for a phone booth. None in view. He started to walk. Then, he started to laugh, for he knew he looked a sight with his slippers and pajama bottoms and this damn toothbrush.

He found a phone booth after two blocks at the end of the business area. He cradled the phone receiver between his ear and shoulder and dropped the quarter from his lips into the coin slot. He dialed 411 with the end of his toothbrush.

"What city?" a recording asked him.

"Thorpe," he barked from the corner of his mouth.

"What listing?" the recording asked.

"Bernard Jessup!"

J. D. waited and listened to the number, memorizing it as only the King of Slugs could. He leaned forward and pressed down the flashhook with his toothbrush and labored to get the other quarter out from under his tongue to between his lips. Finally he deposited the quarter and dialed the Jessup phone number with his toothbrush and anxiously waited. First ring—no answer; second ring—no answer. During the third ring: "Come on, " he muttered.

Then, "Hello," Ashlee answered in a sleepy voice.

"Ashlee, this is J. D. Don't hang up," he said in a garbled voice before letting the toothbrush drop out of his mouth.

"Are you in the hospital?"

"Never mind that. I'm at your bank in Thorpe." He waited out the long pause.

"What are you..are you crazy?"

"Yer Gawd-damn right I am. So you better get down here with the keys to let me in or I'll do somethin' real crazy like call in a story to the Hannibal paper about the Jerome teacher who had an affair with the man who sold Kedloe's land to Stone."

"I'll be there," she said.

"Ashlee! I need a few things. Some baggy pants, a hat, and a flashlight. And a pair of socks."

He breathed a sigh of relief after he let the phone receiver drop. With the key behind his lower lip, he walked gingerly toward the bank.

Later, inside Ashlee's parked car in front of the Thorpe Bank, Ashlee was helping J. D. put on a pair of jogging pants and socks while they talked from her front seat.

"Whatever you find in there I don't want my family brought into this," she insisted.

"Does your dad blame himself for…"

"What his father did?" she snapped. "For foreclosing on a man who murdered three dozen innocent people who were mostly children?"

She finished dressing J. D. by putting a baseball cap on his head.

"How could you let me make all of those wasted calls?"

"My father made me promise never to disclose anything to anybody about that box! Can you see that? Huh? Do you know how hard it was on me to see you up in that tree all day?"

J. D. swallowed hard. "Let's go."

Ashlee unlocked the old bank's front door and led the way inside with the flashlight to the safe deposit box area. She shone the light on the box marked #78. J. D. worked the key from inside his mouth to his lips. She held her hand out for him to drop the key onto her palm. But then, she took it from his lips and wiped it off on her shirt sleeve. He intently watched her insert the key into the box lock, turn the key, and slide out the rusty safe deposit box.

"That's it!" he excitedly whispered.

He followed her light to a small private booth that had a dusty chair that he sat on. She placed the safe deposit box in front of him on a counter.

"Will you help me with this?" he said.

He watched her open the box while shining the light on it with her other hand. First, Ashlee found a 3 x 5 index card inside the box that they read silently together.

"Both God and the devil are spirit persons, forms of life higher than humans and unseen to your eyes."

Ashlee put the card down on the counter and removed a land deed from the box that she and J. D. studied.

"It's the original deed to the Kedloe land," J. D. whispered.

Next, Ashlee removed a large envelope from inside the box. She opened the sealed envelope and took out two hundred thousand dollars in hundred-dollar bills along with a note that she read out loud after he asked her to.

"Jack, I trust the Jessup family to give the contents of this box to you only when the land across the road from my house is safe and never sold to anyone in your lifetime. The Jessups are the only people who know of this box. Bernard Jessup owned this bank in 1927 and is not responsible for that devil's cowardly deed that hurt so many people in our town. I know Mr. Jessup carried a lot of guilt to his grave, a guilt I know so well."

"I hope this tax-free gift of two hundred thousand dollars will carry you through till age 50 and that you'll never sell the land across the road. If the land is ever sold, I want you to give this money to the survivors at Sunnyside. Know that I always love you, Grandpa Dunn."

Ashlee folded up the letter and J. D. swallowed hard. It was as if they both could hear him reading his letter. Next, Ashlee took out the sealed letter that was in young Ray's back pocket the day of the disaster. She opened it. The letter was addressed to "My Favorite Teacher."

Ashlee shone the light on it as they read it silently together, hearing young Ray's voice. The letter was dated May 17, 1927, the night before the disaster. The letter read:

"Dear Teacher, my plan is to get to know you. I, too, have been watching and admiring you from above. Last night I made a vow to ask you if I may come to school today. Now that I have asked you on this beautiful day in May, and have seen your smile, I will leave this letter for you at school today. My work here will be finished soon. If you can meet me for lunch today at the café, I will feel most honored and fortunate to share your company during this Spring of our lives. Sincerely yours, Raymond Dunn."

They are both touched by Ray's letter as Ashlee opened that last envelope and article in the box. It was a letter addressed to J. D. and dated Christmas Day, five years ago. They read it together silently in Ray's voice.

"J. D., a few days before the school disaster I was in the basement of the Jerome School checking on the school's phone system. I smelled gun powder. It turned out to be the dynamite Kedloe had rigged throughout the school's foundation. I only put this together after the fact."

"See, I was the first person on the scene when the school blew up. I found my favorite teacher dead, under the rubble, and she was clutching two dead children in her arms. It was so obvious that she was protecting them, it was a sight I can never forget."

"I felt so guilty for not investigating the smell of powder that I bought the Kedloe land and the land across the road where my house is. I never told your father anything except that I helped after the disaster. I've spent most of my life protecting the same people I know I could have saved. This was a terrible thing to bear and to keep secret all these years. I envied your life, living anywhere you chose. I chose to stay here and save my money for all those children I could have saved."

"I know my frugal ways were hard on your grandmother and your father. It made your father not want to spend much time around me after he left home. I do understand that. Perhaps that's what I wanted, to be a miser that would push my son away so he would not have to live with this guilt too. I'm so sorry to your father and grandmother for this selfish life of mine half-lived. I hope you can understand all this. Love, Grandpa Dunn."

They cried together. He let his head fall forward and sobbed. She put down the light and rubbed the back of his neck tenderly. They both knew so clearly that they had come from people who unconsciously gave them this miasmic pool of guilt, a guilt that kept their swirling, unlived lives muted to joy and unable to truly love. The Jessups and Dunns, the survivors and the dead, were all one—Ashlee, J. D., and their parents, were all heaped onto the same flaming pile of sinister brutality that could never burn off completely. This kind of terribleness Kedloe had done was more than any rescuer could save in the rubble. Now J. D. realized what Kedloe had done—and what was done to all people who cherished safety for their children. And his evil deed would go beyond the last survivor, just as it had reached himself and the woman crying while rubbing his neck. Kedloe had found a way to keep hurting all people through Ed Stone, by showing us his path of destruction again and again and again.

Even at this very moment, when box #78 had revealed so much more understanding for two more of the children—another survivor was gone.

Devils Will Die Today

"Sir, are you related to Mr. Linn?" the nurse asked.

"No, no relation," Pell returned from his chair in the hospital waiting room.

From his years of training at listening to people, he sensed bad news.

"Is Mr. Linn going to recover?" he asked, blinking once.

"No. He passed away a few minutes ago," she said.

She could see the news sink into his chest and cause his shoulders to droop a bit. Pell didn't hear her kind words before she turned and left the waiting room. He thought he heard her say that Hannibal police would be here soon to get his statement. His mind had been on something he had thought of upon hearing of Mr. Linn's death—a vast majority of the Jerome Disaster survivors had no children; the ones that did have children, few had more than one child. He had first discovered this in Tecumseh, a town inhabited by large Irish/Catholic families. At the time, he sloughed it off as a national trend when today families are smaller.

He walked out of the hospital lobby and waited for the police by Albert's car. He returned the keys to the ignition and pondered his dilemma.

"Should I tell them that Mr. Linn died because he thought he saw Kedloe?" he asked himself.

Soon, he figured out that if he stayed to give his statement to the authorities, he would make Kedloe and the man responsible for Missouri Madness a household word. This is not what he wanted now. He had made his decision. With his pocket hanky, he wiped Albert's door handles inside and out, the keys and steering wheel, all free of his fingerprints. He was sure the nurse and cab driver hadn't recognized him. He could not risk a cab now. He started to walk toward the lights of a convenience store.

As he walked, he knew it would be dawn in a few hours. It was too far to walk back to Jerome and get his rental car. Now, he was glad the rental car was registered in his agent's name. The further he walked away from the hospital, the more he wanted to just keep walking. He looked back several times and did not see any police vehicles arriving to get his statement. He was sure it would be criminal, perhaps a felony, to leave without giving an account for a police officer's death. They would know there was no foul play in the matter. He had to call his attorney, who was also his agent.

"He would know what I should do," he told himself calmly.

Then, as if to affirm it, he smiled and said aloud: "Richard will know."

She descended the stairs on the way back to her parents' kitchen in Thorpe. This place was so familiar to her, more so than her apartment. She was raised in this house, and yet, she knew the man sitting at her kitchen table, still dressed in his hospital pajama bottoms and slippers with the cab driver's shirt that smelled of stale tobacco, is the first man other than a family member who has ever been inside this house to visit her.

"That's odd," she thought.

He turned on a small radio that was flush against the wall with a toaster and full napkin holder; then, he quickly turned it off upon seeing the cut-out newspaper article about Cochrand's death—the headline: "Florida Man Dies Near Missouri Madness."

He was into the article when she entered the kitchen carrying a bottle of Excedrin pain reliever. She got him a glass of water from a water purifier mounted on the sink. To her, he looked so down when he finished reading the article.

"How many do you want?"

"What kind is it?"

"Excedrin," she said.

"Oh, good, that's what David Jansen used. Remember him? The Fugitive. He looked like he always had a headache, didn't he?"

She was still smiling waiting for an answer, showing him the bottle of Excedrin.

"Four, that should be enough," he said.

She started to give him one capsule at a time with the water, holding one capsule in front of his lips.

"All four at once," he said.

She put the four capsules to his lips. He took them all with one gulp of water she poured slowly over his lips. He looked into her eyes as if he trusted her, then swallowed the four capsules.

"Thanks," he said.

"You're welcome."

He picked up the article about Cochrand. "Cochrand was doing what I should've done."

She went behind him and started to rub his neck and spoke softly to him. "Don't blame yourself. Remember what Ray said about blame and guilt for what Kedloe did."

"Yeah, but he sure didn't stop blaming himself, did he?"

"No, I suppose he didn't. But what kind of life was that? As long as a survivor knows that damn place is there, suffering continues, no matter how much money it takes in," Ashlee said.

"Is it possible that the awareness of it, I mean, all the people that see it today, somehow deter it from happening again?"

She went around to face him. Looking into her eyes he knew what her answer was.

"I know this is something that won't happen again in Jerome, but I know there's a chance it could impress some psychotic tourist out there who would know how terrible he could make things for his school or town that he hates as much as Kedloe did. There is an element out there who prefers bad attention over no attention. Our society breeds those cowards more than any country on earth. And if one of them copied Kedloe and blamed it on Missouri Madness, it would only give Stone more publicity and more idiots that want to see the damn place."

"You may be right, Ashlee, but it's like Jerome has been waiting for this to come along. The town hasn't grown or moved on. The people have just let this happen. Maybe it's really what they want, some kind of attention finally for what Kedloe did to them. Is that possible?"

"I would like you to go with me on my route after you're feeling better."

"I have no desire to see those people. At least now that's the way I feel."

"Okay," she said.

He winced from pain while getting to his feet.

"I'll take you to the hospital tomorrow," she said.

"No, you won't. I'll go to my own doctor."

Just then, he turned on the table radio and moved the tuner looking for a news station.

"You think your escape made the news?" she laughed.

"No," he smiled, not wanting to alarm her about the incident with Albert's patrol car during his cab ride. Merle Haggard's song "That's the Way Love Goes" was playing on the radio.

"Leave it there! I love that song!" she cried, then she went over and stood in front of him, wanting to slow-dance with him. Sensing his protest, she said softly, "Music and dance are healing."

She gently placed his bandaged hands on her waist, then she carefully laid the palms of her hands on his shoulders near the back of his neck. Very slowly they danced, turned slowly while looking into each other's eyes until the song ended; all the while each knew they had shared something in that bank tonight that would bond them and begin their healing.

When the song was over, he reached down and shut off the radio. If anything happened to Albert—tomorrow was a better time to hear about it, he thought.

"How 'bout a very hot bath?" she smiled.

"With you?" he smiled back in obvious pain.

She nodded yes, and he painfully, in slow-motion as both of them were laughing, tried to kiss her.

"Even my hair hurts," he laughed.

She removed the baseball cap she brought him and touched his hair that was burned down to his bare scalp in many spots.

Upstairs in Ashlee's bedroom, he sat on the side of her king-size bed near the bedside table in the dark. He watched her sitting on the side of the tub while she prepared the temperature just right for their bath water. He had watched her pour in bubble bath after she had lit several candles in several places in the large bathroom.

He wanted to be with her now, but the thought of Geronimo in the hospital and not letting her know about what he saw in the cab bothered him. Above the running water, he called her name. She came over to him and sat beside him, looking at him with those intelligent eyes.

"When I was in that cab on the way to your bank, I saw a man driving Albert's patrol car."

"Where was Albert?"

"I didn't see Albert. The man asked the cab driver for directions to the hospital."

She asked him why he didn't tell her sooner as she went over to her bedside phone and dialed Albert's phone number.

As the phone rang: "I didn't think about it until downstairs."

She replaced the receiver after no answer. Then, she got a phone book out of a drawer and riffed through the Yellow Pages looking for the hospital in Hannibal as he was now thinking about whether he should tell her about the journalist from England, Mr. Pell, and how he thought he resembled Kedloe. And how he had stopped over at his house to talk to him one night.

Ashlee waited on the phone for any information regarding Albert being admitted to the hospital. All J. D. could think about was himself and how he wanted to have her now in that candlelit bubble bath. The urge to scream it to her was inchoate, lodged deep in his throat and itching to get out like the burns under his bandages. Overcome by dizziness, he had to stand and move around because David Jansen's pain killer was making his heart beat so fast.

He went to the running bath and watched the water rise slowly in the flickering light as Ashlee's voice raced his heart faster. "No, I'm not a relative! I'm a close friend, very close friend, and he's not answering his phone! I need to know if he's there or not! If he's there, I'll come down! Do you understand?" she yelled into the phone.

She listened to the hospital receptionist tell her again about hospital policy regarding releasing information on patients.

Ashlee slammed down the receiver. He knew he shouldn't say this, but it just occurred to him.

"I can't go down there. They'll want to admit me."

"Well, I've got to go down there."

His head was spinning on Excedrin rushes and all the things that might happen if she went to the hospital now.

"Just do me a favor," he said, walking slowly over to her as she prepared to leave the room as soon as she found her keys. "Don't mention I saw the man driving his car or anything until I sort this out."

"I'll just say I was concerned, because I called.."

She couldn't think of a reason why she'd be calling him at this hour. He couldn't either. Then, J. D. told Ashlee that he'd better go with her.

"You need your rest. I can go alone," she said.

"I want to go. Can I get a shirt and some loose pants? This shirt stinks."

After he removed the shirt, she took it from him and told him she'd throw it out.

"No you won't. I paid a hundred bucks for that shirt."

He waited near the convenience store pay phones for his cab he had just called. He rocked back and forth on his feet, going over the orders his attorney gave him just minutes earlier and after he had told his attorney everything that happened.

"Take a cab to the rental car in Jerome. Drive to the St. Louis airport and keep your mouth shut. I'll handle the statement later," his attorney told him.

Then he started to tell his attorney that he didn't think he should be leaving town if it was a crime to do so for not leaving a statement, especially since a policeman was dead. His attorney's final words were still ringing in his ear before he hung up on his client.

"You don't think is correct. I do your thinking now. Call me from LAX and I'll pick you up, okay?"

"Okay," he said.

He had to do what his attorney told him to do in this kind of matter. After all, he was not a U. S. citizen, and even though his reputation as a good man was important to him, he could be ignorant of the law and probably not be prosecuted.

"Besides," he assured himself, "I did nothing wrong; I tried to help the man. I did all that I could."

Just then his cab arrived. Trouble. What are the odds of this? he thought, as he hurried to the cab's back door. It was the same cab driver who had given him directions to the hospital. They recognized each other right off, no doubt about that or any use in pretending they hadn't met earlier.

It was too late to get another cab, for he had committed himself; now he would keep his mouth shut.

"You did find the hospital, sir?" the driver smiled into his rear-view mirror, now wearing a black T-shirt.

"Yes, thank you."

The driver waited, his eyes going back and forth to his mirror. He was waiting for his fare to tell him where he wanted to go. But Pell's mind was on the fact that this man would be a witness against him if he left town now without giving a statement. He had to decide right now if he was going to do what his attorney ordered him to do.

"Sir? Where to?"

"Oh yes, yes, uh, first..to the Ramada, then, to Jerome."

As the cab started to back away from the convenience store, he thought of the fact that his attorney never told him to go to his room to get his belongings. Now, this man could identify him, where he was staying, the rental car in Jerome; it was all turning so messy.

"On second thought, could you drive me over to the hospital emergency entrance and wait for me a bit?"

"How long of a wait?"

"Oh, shouldn't be too terribly long. I have to give a statement to the authorities."

"No problem," the driver said.

Two unmarked Hannibal Police vehicles were parked near Albert's patrol car when he stepped out of his cab's back seat. He would have to use his real name and hope for the best.

"Honesty is the best policy," he said to himself. He smiled as he approached two detectives who were talking to the same nurse who told him Mr. Linn had died. The nurse was apparently describing the man she now saw walking toward her. He would be able to declare his name away from the nurse, he hoped.

"Yes, I believe you gentlemen are here for my statement?" he smiled.

As he had hoped, the detectives ushered him into a private waiting room away from the nurse.

J. D. could see the same cab driver who took him to Thorpe waiting near Albert's patrol car outside the emergency entrance while Ashlee went inside to find out about Albert. The pain from the burns on his hands gave his whole body this itchy hotness feeling that made it difficult for him to sit still. He was thinking about how he wanted to go with Ashlee mainly because his safe deposit box was in the trunk of her car. All that money and he trusted nobody with it. Then he would be thinking why in the world would that man be driving Albert's car?

It must have been ten or fifteen minutes later when he saw Ashlee exit the hospital. He could tell something bad had happened; it was obvious in her walk, and she was crying. He watched her face until she got behind the wheel, staring straight ahead, stunned. He waited.

"Albert's dead," she said finally, without looking at J. D., shaking her head in disbelief. "He's gone. He had a heart attack while he was parked in his patrol car. And he died."

Just then, J. D. saw the journalist come out of the hospital with the two detectives. He watched them chat for a few minutes and handshake.

"Ashlee, see that man getting into the cab? He's the man I saw driving Albert's car. He came to my house and asked me questions about Kedloe and my grandpa. He's a dead ringer for Kedloe. I'll bet that's got something to do with Albert's heart attack."

She couldn't see his face and wouldn't know anyway if he
looked like Kedloe because she'd never seen a photo of Kedloe.
When the cab drove away with Pell, "Follow that cab," he told
Ashlee.

At the Hannibal Ramada: From a hundred yards away, they
watched him get out of the cab and hustle into his room on the first
floor, leaving the back door of the cab open as if he was returning.
"He's leaving again," J. D. said.
"I have to talk to him," Ashlee said, as she was about to
drive over to the cab and confront him.
"No, stay here," J. D. insisted.
"I have to know what happened."
Just then, he came out of his room carrying his suitcase,
which he put on the back seat of the cab before he got in. They
followed the cab.
She talked about how she couldn't believe Albert was
gone. He said nothing, keeping his eyes on the cab taillights; his
hands hurt terribly because the pain killer had worn off
completely.
"He's going to Jerome," he said.
"He must have checked out with the police," she said.
"His rental car must be in Jerome," J. D. surmised.
"Well, either way, we've got to talk to him now. We can't
just keep following him around," she said.
"Yeah," he agreed.
They stayed closer to the cab as it pulled into the Middle
School's parking lot and parked next to his rental car.
"Park next to his car," J. D. said.
The cab driver saw the man with the toothbrush get out of
the car.
"You know that guy?" he asked after the man with the
British accent paid him.
"Yes, I believe I do," he said, curious about the bandages
on Mr. Dunn's hands.
J. D. smiled at the cab driver as he and Ashlee waited

beside the stranger's rental car. The driver took his time, for he thought he recognized his fare as a celebrity, staying parked and calling in to his dispatcher as Ashlee pressed the man before he could ask J. D. what happened to his hands.

"I'm a friend of Albert Linn, the police officer. I need to know what happened. You were with him."

The stranger unlocked the trunk of his rental car to put his suitcase inside. He was thinking about what to tell this woman. When he slammed the trunk down, he turned to her and looked into her sad eyes. He could see she recognized him or was close.

"Is there a place nearby we can get a cup of coffee?" the man asked them.

J. D. intervened, pointing down the hill to the Jerome Café. "Yeah, there's a café just down there that should be opening about now."

"Shall we walk?" the stranger smiled.

They flanked him as they crossed the road onto the Old School grounds. Grass dew flecked the tops of their shoes as they walked slowly; then, he stopped and told them exactly what happened in Albert's patrol car, and that he believed his resemblance to the madman triggered his heart attack.

"You do resemble Kedloe," J. D. said as they continued on their walk down the hill toward the café.

"I've been told that," he said, his hands in both pants pockets.

When Ashlee remembered his name, he said:

"I didn't tell the police that Mr. Linn thought he saw Kedloe. That can't be proven. It's only probable. I'm not a journalist. I'm an actor, here to find out if I can play Kedloe on film."

J. D. and Ashlee remembered seeing this man in several films. They never said his name in his presence.

"But since I've been here, I don't believe I should play him. And I don't believe what he did to the people here should be on film."

"Mr. Pell," J. D. smiled, as they neared the café that was just opening, "what made you decide that?" he asked.

"Two things, well three if you count Mr. Linn. When I went to Tecumseh, I discovered that Kedloe was already a killer in his youth."

"His stepmother," J. D. said.

"Yes, and I know if I played his character, I would have to play anger and rage with absolutely no other emotions."

"I've seen you play that," Ashlee said as they entered the café and sat down at the back of the café with Pell purposely sitting with his back to the room.

"Yes, but this is about reality with real survivors."

"You said there were two reasons," J. D. said.

"Yes. Mr. Cochrand. I heard him when he gave his piece of mind to Mr. Stone. I couldn't shake the image of that day when he looked under all those blankets for his son."

"So, it is the kind of story that's too terrible to tell?" Ashlee said.

"Yes."

"What about this Missouri Madness of Stone's?" she asked him.

"It's deplorable. Tastless pure greed exploiting a town's pain."

"Have you taken the tour?" J. D. asked him.

"No, I have no desire to now."

The waitress brought them coffee. Ashlee noticed how the actor avoided eye contact with the waitress.

"It must be hard to be famous and get around like this," she said, after the waitress left.

"It's part of my life," he smiled.

"I know Albert wanted to close down Stone's operation. His role as the protector for the survivors was a big part of his life," she said.

"I wish there was something I could do to help," the man said.

There was a long pause. When J. D. looked into Ashlee's eyes, some kind of synergistic spark between them had manifested a sudden impulse to give this famous actor a chance to be a protagonist in the real world. It was as if Albert and Ray were

now working through Ashlee and J. D. to end this madness.
Ashlee smiled at J. D. before turning to Mr. Pell.

"You mean that?"

"What?"

"That you wish there was something you could do to help."

"Yes, of course."

"You'll need a disguise," J. D. smiled, removing the cap
Ashlee gave him, putting it on the actor's head. They all laughed
when she turned the cap around backwards. They laughed louder
when the actor turned and angled the bill of the cap sideways
between his ear and temple. "What are you suggesting?" he
asked, winding down his laughter.

Ashlee's answer left him gaping. "Help us destroy that
place."

At first, he snorted as if they were joking, then he asked
them if they were joking. He could see they were dead serious.
Pell returned J. D.'s hat to his head, covering his bad haircut from
the fire.

"I'm expected to arrive in L. A. today."

"Make a call," J. D. smiled and returned the cap to the
actor's head with the bill of the cap low, shading those intelligent
eyes that were blue and thinking and thinking, until he said:

"What if the detectives break their word and leak my
involvement with Mr. Linn? I couldn't stay around here."

"You'll need a good disguise," Ashlee smiled. Then,
leaning closer to the actor, "We're the only ones that know what
really happened."

"Is this blackmail?" Pell smiled, shifting his jaw and
shifting his lower teeth while looking from side to side at Ashlee,
then J. D.

"No," J. D. laughed. "And I'm sure that cab driver was
never even mentioned as a witness who could verify giving you
two rides and meeting us in Jerome at your rental car before flying
to L. A."

He knew they had him, at least it looked like they did. His
best performance, he smiled inwardly, though he admired them for
this. Besides, he wanted to help them.

"I have to make a call," he told them.

When they got up to leave, the actor pulled the cap's bill down, hiding his eyes.

Later, Ashlee and the actor chatted in J. D.'s doctor's waiting area as J. D. got his neck adjusted by his Hannibal chiropractor, popping left, then right.

The actor was on the phone in Ashlee's kitchen while J. D. and Ashlee waited in her living room. They could hear him talking to his attorney.

"Look, I'm not returning today. It's too late for that. I've given my statement to the detectives. They assured me that my name will be left out of it. I'm staying here. In Thorpe, Missouri. With friends. Their names aren't important. I want you to tell the studio I pass on the offer. Yes, that's right. I don't want anything to do with the project. I don't care about that. Yes, that's final. I know I've been wrong before, but not this time. Phone number here? I don't wish to give it out. The tabloids? I'll deal with that if it comes. Good day, Richard."

When he entered the living room, she was giving J. D. Excedrin and pouring water for him so he could swallow four tablets.

"You really should get back to the hospital," he advised J. D.

"I will, when it's over."

He sat down across from them on an antique velvet divan of her grandparents. He started stroking the dark chocolate colored velvet on the armrest when he told them that he cannot be involved with anything of a criminal nature that would hurt his career in any way whatsoever. He asked them if they were clear on this matter. They nodded their agreement, a bit awed that here in Thorpe was this celebrity, crossing his legs and sitting back comfortably not five feet from them, patting his shirt pocket and telling them he was going outside for a smoke and a stroll around the block. He stood up so gracefully, every movement precise and effortless, using as little energy as possible. He left them thinking about a way to destroy Stone's Missouri Madness legally.

The greens of the magnolias lined both sides of the street. He walked away from the main business district. He had seen the Thorpe Bank when he first arrived in the area. The bank was at the top of his list of places to see. He knew all about the banker Jessup who felt responsible for Kedloe's deed. Ashlee was on his list, too. It wasn't important to tell her what he knew, for he was getting so close to manifesting his dream. And if he hadn't given J. D. Thorpe Bank by sending in the elderly Mrs. Bordon into his hospital room, his dream would be as dead as Mr. Cochrand.

Rounding the corner two blocks away from the Jessup house, he smiled and chuckled out loud at this plot he'd created, far better so far than any script he'd ever read. He had no idea where it was going or if it was going at all.

He lit a Rothman from its blue and white package that a screenwriter friend from Canada had sent him. He had sent along two cartons with his screenplay. That's what finally brought him here. His friend wrote it for him in mind to play Kedloe, and knew why he would consider it. If he played the role in the script, he'd be found out and stripped of all his dignity he'd worked so hard to create. If he didn't play Kedloe, there was a good chance the film would never be made. Or, he could do one cut-throat business move that wasn't all that rare in the business.

His friend up north was loyal and true; he had no reservations about that. Seven million dollars to play that madman would be his biggest payday to date, if he signed the contract his attorney anxiously had waiting on top of his desk.

He thought about how Kedloe destroyed an entire town for a few hundred dollars in hated tax money to be assessed, as Pell puffed deeply on his Canadian cigarette. But this, this partnership with J. D. and Ashlee, he mused, could be the most important role of his life. He had been involved with projects where the script was hammered out day by day while on location. Very precarious stuff, but some of his best work came on the fly, he smirked, remembering one of his early films when he delivered his lines that had been written on napkins just a half hour earlier.

After his second smoke, he scratched his rough face stubble and put on a pair of sunglasses from his shirt pocket, then pulled down the bill of the cap to the top of the frames. He would hear what they thought and see where it led. For he knew he had a way out if it all failed—he would leave.

They talked him into taking Stone's tour. J. D. paid close attention to the reaction on the actor's face when he stood before the mannequin of Kedloe. From behind his sunglasses and cap, he knew right off that he had an uncanny resemblance to the killer. Kedloe's jowls even sagged in the same places as his, with the left side having the same indented dimple. The face of Kedloe was more stern, menacing, and of course the eyes were dead, but the shape of his skull matched his, along with the wisp of gray/brown hair combed back, exposing the same slanting forehead.

But, no one knew what Kedloe looked like, except for the seniors around here who would never go to a film about the disaster, he thought. He was yet rationalizing, as if he had signed on to do the picture.

"You do," Ashlee whispered to Pell.

The actor grunted softly and clasped his hands behind his back, twiddling his thumbs. That's odd, he said to himself. I've never in my life put my hands behind my back and twiddled my thumbs. He knew from his body language expression training that it meant his hands were tied and he had no clue how to get out of the situation.

The threesome left the tour; they stood in front of the Kedloe house, staring at the house as if gauging how it could be destroyed. Soon, they headed toward the rental car parked on J. D.'s land across the road. The rubble of the Dunn house was sickening to J. D., causing the skin under his bandages to itch terribly as they walked across the road. He asked Ashlee if she'd see if he had any mail in his mailbox. There was one piece of mail—a letter from Stone's office. He told her to open it and to read it out loud as all three stood beside the rental car. J. D.

listened while staring blankly at the blackened remains of Oz, burnt to a crisp like some massive log.

Stone's letter was an invitation for J. D. to name his price for his grandfather's land, land he wanted to buy from J. D. in a bad way. They all thought that Stone had burned down the Dunn house. After being in the Thorpe Bank, Ashlee and J. D. both knew that this land would never be sold to anyone, ever, as long as that cold-hearted place across the road was there. J. D. told her to tear up Stone's letter. She did.

Later that afternoon, they sat at a table in the Country Swing bar. J. D. thought they should get drunk and brainstorm, mainly because he wanted to numb his brain and feel no pain. Pell wore his sunglasses and the cap, his beard stubble now a more pronounced grizzled gray. After Ashlee convinced Pell he should stay at her house with them, J. D. said:

"The guard makes it impossible to do anything at night."

"Couldn't he be distracted?" Ashlee asked.

After she and J. D. went back and forth about the security guard and ways of distracting him, their partner thought he should lead them in the only safe direction.

"What if the survivors destroyed it?"

Ashlee and J. D. sat looking at each other, thinking about that possibility.

"They'd have a good chance at getting away with it," J. D. said.

"No one would prosecute them," Ashlee smiled, her spirits lifted.

They leaned in closer to hear the actor's soft, trained voice.

"Now we may be onto something here. I suggest we knock it around a bit."

"Idea!" Ashlee blurted.

Pell hushed her with his finger to his lips. "What if I hauled a vanload of the survivors from Sunnyside over to Kedloe's..."

"They'd never go there," J. D. interrupted.

"Let me finish. If they went at night with gasoline and matches, the guard couldn't stop them all."

"The guard would have to be stopped from calling the fire department or they'd just put it out," Pell said.

"Wouldn't Stone just rebuild it with insurance money?" Pell asked. Then he added: "Not with enough negative press coverage."

Ashlee informed Pell that J. D. had the original deed to the Kedloe land.

"I'm not sure, I'd have to check with my attorney; but, if you could get Stone to accept money for the land and prove it with a receipt, " Pell said pensively and added, "Stone would get his investment back from the insurance money."

"This sounds too complicated," J. D. said. "I don't want anything to do with frauding an insurance company."

"I don't either," Pell said.

"Albert's funeral is in two days. I want this all over before then. At least that's what I want," she said.

"Why's that?" J. D. asked, then finished his seventh shot of whiskey by lowering his head to the shot glass and sipping fast through a sip stick straw. They waited for her answer.

"I just do, that's all. I don't know if I can do this later."

Pell and Ashlee cut themselves off while J. D. was determined to get drunk. Ashlee told J. D. that Stone will have to get his money back that he paid J. D. for the Kedloe land.

"No problem," he replied.

"I do think you should go back to the hospital," Ashlee told him. "And we should go."

"They said I should go to Iowa City and get my hands done," J. D. said when Ashlee stood up.

She sat back down. "Who said?"

"Doctors."

Then he laughed out his words in a drunken stupor. "They asked me what kind of work I do. I told them I was a telemarketer. They said I may never be able to dial a phone again if I don't go to Iowa City. I said that might be a good thing," he laughed alone. Ashlee and Mr. Pell knew what should be done.

"J. D., I'll drive you to Iowa City. It can't be too far off," Pell said.

"I'll go with you," Ashlee said.

The King of Slugs was serious when he told them no, that they had to get Stone first and that he could go to Iowa City when that was done.

Pell winked his idea at Ashlee as J. D. bent to sip out of his empty shot glass.

"One more for the road," Pell smiled.

Next morning, he woke up with a hangover, for two hours unwilling to open his eyes. J. D. kept falling in and out of disjointed dreams that his subconscious mind was trying to connect. WY, the abbreviation for Wyoming, or did it mean why? This WY was shown to him in these dreams while sleeping on the floor of Oz in the middle of the afternoon. In the dream, he had balled his socks and thrown them high up into the bare brown branches of Oz though it was in summertime. He watched the socks coming down, bouncing from one branch to the other—all the time aware that the Kedloe land across the road was barren with no sign of Missouri Madness. The Kedloe ground was untouched as when he was a boy. But he wasn't a boy in these dreams because he could not have tossed his socks so high up into the branches of Oz unless he had the strength of a man's arm. And this Pell/actor was a specious thing to him—the name and the profession a true lie that kept coming to him right behind or ahead of the WY. Ashlee was not in these dreams, and neither was Albert or his Grandpa Dunn.

He was about to open his eyes; but first, he went over in his mind the shots in these dreams—the wide trunk of Oz and its branches; the tumbling balled socks; Kedloe's barren land; the WY, Pell/actor; and that ominous summer/hot breeze blowing on his face and howling around his ear, only one ear. And all those shots over and over, spanning real hours yet for only seconds, mere flashes behind his will to not want to see or open his eyes to what was there. Just then, for a second, he thought he could remember something he heard while passed out on Pell's back seat. But he lost it, now lost forever in this alcohol that was destroying brain cells one by one, those cells that have the ability to recall a dream were the first ones to die.

It was time to open his eyes. When he did, he could not figure out exactly where he was. He knew he was now in a hospital bed and could feel that his bandages had been changed. But how did he get here? he wondered. Would they admit me drunk without even knowing who I was, for God's sake? he asked himself.

The last thing he remembered was falling face-first onto the back seat of Pell's rental car. Now, from the slits of light he allowed onto his tender eyeballs, he knew for certain he was on a hospital bed. But where? Hannibal? Iowa City? The curtains were closed, the room was dark; his eyes hurt to look at the slivers of sunlight along the curtain edges. His mind raced along the waves of treachery and deceit—where was his money in his safe deposit box? Where were they?

Once again he wore hospital-green as he got to his bare feet and painfully made his way over to the window. He raked open the curtains. Sprawled out before him was this massive splay of university buildings arranged so neatly into these rolling knolls and this network of roads with traffic creeping along as only in Iowa.

He craned his throbbing skull and scanned the parking lot below, looking for Pell's rental car from his sixth-floor room. He knew he had to be in Iowa City.

He thought about how the doctors in Hannibal told him if he didn't come here to get skin grafts, his fingers would be like fins and he'd be unable to bend and flex them. That thought was what kept him from bolting out of there right now. He would wait.

From his hospital bed, he pushed a service call button. He waited. And while he waited, it dawned on him that he would miss Albert's funeral tomorrow. He was anxious to find out if Ashlee was still here. And the thought of that actor staying with her in her house alone made his hands and wrists itch terribly. And he thought about how it was strange to him that nothing was mentioned about Albert's death in the Jerome Café the next morning when they were there.

His suspicions heightened when a nurse finally answered his call. She told J. D. that Pell and Ashlee left word with her to tell him they'd be back in three days after his surgery.

"Three days?" he queried his nurse. "When is my surgery scheduled?" he asked her.

"Tomorrow morning," she smiled.

"Tomorrow?"

"Your left hand," she said.

"Can't both hands be done tomorrow?"

"I don't know. You'll have to ask your doctor," she said.

"Who's my doctor?"

"Dr. Whitsell."

"Don't you have to sign in when you're admitted, or sign papers to have surgery?"

"Your wife signed for you."

He looked away from the nurse when he asked her if she would help him make a phone call.

He was on the phone with the Hannibal newspaper for at least a half-hour at the nurse's station. When he returned to his room, he paced back and forth from the window to the door for a good hour. He was stuck on the fact that there was no notice of Albert's death or any obituary for Albert Linn.

He stopped pacing, looked down at his bandaged hands and with silent acrid asperity, he let fly in his mind anything that came, anything that might brainstorm him into clarity in his helplessness as he continued to pace: You call the operator, ask them what time it is and they won't tell you; they give you this recorded message to call. What the hell is this? Just tell me what time it is for Christ's sake? WY?

"WY?" he repeated out loud. "What the hell does WY mean? WY?" he said louder while going over to the window.

He yanked open the curtains, then, he consciously relaxed, whereupon he could see his first "dream" with clarity. It was when he was a young man fresh out of high school. He wanted to be a poet, perhaps a songwriter. His English teacher, Mr. Patton, always gave him an "A" on every paper he turned in, often reading Jack's work to the class while Jack blushed and squirmed at his desk. It was the attention that made him blush. Would he be found out and revealed to peers who were into their heads about music, sex, college, Vietnam, more sex, more music, the next game, the weekend. His first poem was titled "The Next Game." He couldn't remember the words to it, yet he could still see Mr. Patton reading it to the class.

Now, as he stood at the window high above Iowa City, the slow melodic pace of traffic was streaming his unconscious to remember "The Next Game." Just then, a remarkable thing happened—Jack Dunn remembered something from his dead past that soon brought forth a wailing cry from long years of suffering that shot from his belly to his throat, his pain dripped its long string of saliva as he recalled "The Next Game" while he kept his gaze on the pace of the Iowa prairie beyond the glass.

"Running home,
to change my clothes,
for shouts of joy
a little pain,
Win or lose,
I walked home
With time between,
The next game."

He closed his tear-filled eyes and thought he could hear his past hit the tile floor. Poetry had saved his life and damaged his relationship with his dad.

In '71 he grew his hair real long and hitchhiked up to Canada when the draft lottery began picking birthdays and deciding who would die in Vietnam. His number was a high three hundred-something, making it unlikely he would be drafted. But he had already run and humiliated his father in their little part of the world with Lion and Rotary Clubs, and Midwest virtues.

He asked himself if he should run now, just as he asked himself so long ago in his youth. He was stupid then, scared like most young men then, so he ran before his number was drawn. It cost him his father and his dream to be a poet.

Now, he looked down from side to side at his hands.
"Tomorrow I'll run," he smiled.

He went back to the bed and tried to get some rest. He could keep his eyes closed but could not shut down his mind about Albert, Ashlee and that actor, Stone, the survivors, Grandpa Dunn, thousands of worthless phone calls, Oz, and his life unlived. He called his nurse for aspirin and soon had his last meal before his surgery. His doctor dropped by and told him he could do both hands tomorrow and that the skin would be grafted from his buttocks. He tried to sleep.

The sun was going down in Iowa City. J. D. had tried to sleep, but he laid in that hospital bed slathered in worry-sweat. He had asked for something to help him sleep and just had taken two capsules of something, he didn't ask what it was. His nurse turned on the television after his request.

For another hour, he laid there staring at the screen without a clue what was on or why he wasn't nodding off to sleep.

Just when he thought he was dropping off and finished about thinking how hungry he was and Albert's missing obituary, the newscaster on the screen had his full attention.

"The Riverboat Queen Casino docked on the Illinois side of the Mississippi River across from Hannibal, Missouri, was evacuated this afternoon after a bomb threat was called in to the casino office. Casino owner Ed Stone was on hand for an interview with Live Cam reporter Margaret Allen."

J. D. blinked several times trying to stay awake as he watched and listened to Stone sharing a mike with the reporter on the Hannibal side of the river. Stone looked upset, and he was, especially when she asked Stone if the bomb scare was related to his Missouri Madness in Jerome.

"Who knows! All I know is that I lost maybe twenty thousand dollars because some nut made a phone call! Whoever did this should be put away for a long time! It's only going to help in Jerome," he smiled.

"But what about the casino?" she asked.

After Stone had angrily stalked away off camera, she looked into the camera and appeared to J. D. that she was speaking to him.

"Is this part of Missouri Madness? Or, is it only some sore loser at the Queen's betting tables? After police dogs found no trace of explosives on the riverboat, it is reported they were then sent to Jerome's Missouri Madness, just to be safe."

It was too late; J. D. could barely keep his eyes open. His mind wanted to get out of there and get back to Jerome before anything happened. He told himself a hundred times that he's gotta get his hands done first.

The next thing he remembered was just before his surgery. It was just before he nodded off from his anesthesia when he peacefully reminded his doctor to do both hands so that he could get out of here. Soon J. D. was there, in the unconscious mind where dreams are made—where anger and love mix to a vertiginous sense of falling into safety or a black void. This was J. D.'s dream as he fell into unconsciousness; falling, falling back into time just as he was turned onto his stomach and his bandages were removed.

In the dream, he somehow had a feeling that he could control where he stopped in time. The brakes were put on at the 17th of May, 1927, the night before the disaster. The place: Kedloe's parlor. Pell was Kedloe, sitting there in his chair fiddling with a metal puzzle he made, just like the one on the mannequin's lap in Stone's Missouri Madness.

His Grandma Dunn was Mrs. Kedloe, the sweet and innocent woman married to a man she never really knew at all. There was no dialog between them as Mrs. Kedloe canned in her kitchen within view of her tinkering husband. Above the sink on the wall were these framed words that were printed between bunches of blackberries and sunflowers: "Build your garden with seeds of hope and nails of honey."

Then, J. D. could read Kedloe's mind as Kedloe sat in his favorite chair. "She knows more about that damned canned fruit than she'll ever know about me," Kedloe smirked.

The next dream image had Kedloe standing behind his

Grandma Dunn pointing a rifle at the back of her head.

The next image he saw was Kedloe dumping his wife's body in a hogchute that night.

The dream continued to the Kedloe farm the next morning as the buttocks flesh of the King of Slugs was lasered off and the grafting begun on his dialing hand.

Just as Kedloe/Pell was exiting his farm, driving one of Stone's school buses, passing under a blood-red latticed pergola at the entrance where the guardshack is, Kedloe gives a perfunctory wave to J. D., who was telemarketing from Oz with a toothbrush in his mouth.

From J. D.'s point of view, he could see the Kedloe house and barn explode from dynamite. With his bandaged hands, he feverishly looked down to his desktop and could see the list and photos of the victims in the Jerome School Disaster Book. Frantically, he dialed zero with the handle-end of his toothbrush as he watched Kedloe drive the school bus toward Jerome.

"Operator, this is an emergency! Give me the Jerome School!"

"I'm sorry," said the operator, "but Ray Dunn is working on the phone line at the school. Please try again later."

Love and Rockets song "So Alive" played as J. D. scrambled down from Oz and ran as fast as he could down the road toward Jerome after he had circled the house looking for his car that was not there. Faster and faster he ran, barely able to see the back of the school bus that was moving further and further away from him.

The medical team in the operating room had to stop the skin grafting because J. D. flinched violently; he was convulsing his muscles and breathing hard because he saw Mr. Cochrand's yowling/plaintive face while the old man was burning alive inside his overturned car.

The Iowa City team continued the grafting after a nurse patted the sweat from their labored-breathing patient's brow and made a remark about the bad dream Mr. Dunn was having.

J. D. was running into Jerome. Kedloe and the bus were out of view as he ran for the Old School looking for his Grandpa

Dunn up a telephone pole, but the school was getting further and further away the more he languorously moved to reach it. He was lunging, crying and yelling without sound and that's when he saw a boy inside of the cupola that was now at the top of the Old School. That boy was Albert. J. D.'s feet turned to lead when he saw Kedloe come marching out of the Old School with all of the old survivors of today, most of them were residents of Sunnyside.

J. D. watched helplessly as Kedloe marched the elderly survivors into Stone's antique school bus, and he now could see that Stone was the bus driver. Then, he saw his Grandpa Dunn as a young man. He was consoling young Albert inside the cupola high atop the school as they cried while they watched Kedloe and the survivors leave in the bus. And then, J. D. was able to move toward the school in a sensorium of silence, walking on air, moving dream-like and unaware of his feet touching the ground. He could sense she was coming out of the Old School's double doors as if he willed her to. He knew it was Ashlee. She was dressed like one of the Jerome teachers in 1927—black, high-neck collared ankle-length muslin dress with six tiny pearl buttons that gave her an air of import and grace as she strolled toward him in black boots with 2-inch heels while opening a pink and white parasol.

As she stepped closer, he could really see her for the first time. She was so beautiful without a trace of vanity. But she walked right past him as if he was invisible to her. Why wasn't she concerned about Kedloe taking off with the survivors, the same people she protected so fervently? And then it hit him right there as she strolled ahead of him down that hill on this perfect day in May. He could not be seen by her—because he was unable to love or be loved.

He could not get any closer than fifty yards to her. It was as if she too was untouchable. Was she unlovable also? he wondered as he watched her stop to remove her high-laced boots, leaving them there on the sidewalk. He kept his eyes on the shoes, when he reached them he bent to pick them up, but they were so heavy he had to put them down. When he looked up to see her, she had vanished. She had to be inside one of the five or six clapboard homes on the street, the only possible places she could've gone.

He knocked on the first door—nothing. Then, he heard the faint crying of a woman coming from inside the back bedroom. He followed the sounds of grief, getting closer to the bedroom so he paused and listened for clues to what was going on in the room. He saw the same ceramic crucifix in his grandfather's house that was now hanging on the wall in front of him in this stranger's house. He couldn't call out Ashlee's name or say anything. Then, the crying just stopped. He held his breath and listened for more clues. Nothing. J. D. became terrified at what he might see in that room. He couldn't move his legs to enter the room.

"Ashlee," he whispered.

He stepped forward to the doorway wanting the woman to be Ashlee. It was not her. It was George Hammon's mother. She was gently removing the plaster from her boy's face, who was in shock, wide-eyed and spooked out of his little mind, staring up to the ceiling as if terrified that it too would come crashing down on him. Little George was so frightened that he was holding onto his mother's breast, squeezing it as she dug out the plaster from his face. She did not and could not see the stranger in her doorway who was frozen with fear while remembering the scarred old man reaching into his grandfather's casket looking for something related to this day. Perhaps the deed to Kedloe's land, he thought.

"Have you seen Ashlee?" he asked the woman. She couldn't hear him. He left her crying for her son; she was letting out the pain in this pitiful plaintive wailing and yowling cries as if it were the pain her little son was too stunned to feel.

J. D. found himself outside the Old School, behind it, where recess was on. A hundred children were running around playing games, yet it was eerily devoid of any sounds except for the sound of his blood beating in his ears.

The last thing he did in this dream was to look up to where the cupola was, where his young Grandpa Dunn and boy Albert were standing together. But now the cupola was gone and there was no sign of them. He cried.

He woke up that early afternoon feeling no pain in the

same hospital room overlooking Iowa City. His hands were bandaged and he had this feeling that all is well; a very strange feeling for him. Every single detail of his dream he could recall. If he had a mirror within view, he would see the light of aliveness in his eyes again. He had lost that light in his late-twenties somewhere between moves to strange cities, dead-end slug jobs, and the realization that he would never know his father.

Right then, he had this craving for pumpkin pie topped with ice cream, and he wanted "to see" Ashlee, really see her for the first time. As he lay there resisting the urge to call a cab, he could see that his money, Ashlee and Grandpa Dunn, Kedloe and Stone, Albert and all of the gawd-damn madness, was tied up in this same bundle of toxic unwillingness to love and be loved—this flat-out rejection to dance and play and really feel what comes along had ruined his life up till now. He could see that it began with Kedloe's father and grandfather's lack of love and their willingness to be mean and brutal by passing it onto their son. They had made this monster and they too would get away with it just as Kedloe did when he blew himself to bits in front of the school, taking more innocent bystanders out of this world, while the survivors cast themselves into a world the King of Slugs knew so well. It was into this reality of mired nothingness, of toxic, bottled emotions that they held onto. These were the aches and pains, the headaches and crying episodes, and the non-feelingness from a thousand broken records playing melodies of fear, guilt and resentment during a symphony of winds that blew in the Midwest seasons, air that filled their lungs with the same old terror again and again every time the circle of life or a new season came 'round again.

He decided to wait for Ashlee to return. She would show with his money and he would be able to pay his sixteen thousand-dollar medical bill and high-tail it outta here, he told himself. His doctor wanted him to stay for another week. No way. He had already given his hide; he wasn't about to give them his time at seven hundred bucks per day. Forget it, he told the doctor; I have no insurance.

The next day was the hardest for J. D. The waiting was

driving him crazy. Will she show tomorrow? kept creeping into
his mind. It wasn't a matter of trust—it was about what was going
on inside him. Now, he was anxious to just let things happen
versus making things happen.

By late afternoon, the day before Ashlee's hoped-for
arrival, Jack Dunn felt that familiar pain under his temples
diminish. He had been thinking of that exact moment he came into
this world. The cold gray steel of forceps had to be used on his
temples to remove him head-first from his mother's womb. It was
as if this sterile hospital room in Iowa City was his safe place to re-
live the cold fact that he did not want to come into this world.

Now, his temples throbbed, but not that painful throbbing
that kept him close to Excedrin. It was a sense-memory pain his
brain subconsciously remembered from the pattern of trauma made
by the chemical reaction he had as a newborn from the ether
breathed in by his mother when they cut her down there, and gave
her powerful drugs to keep her from feeling what her baby would.

"This crazy world," he muttered.

During his birth, it was in this maelstrom stupor, this all-
out assault by medicine on his safe place, where his problems
began, he knew.

"They didn't need forceps," he muttered.

Until the light went out behind his closed curtains, when
the sun went down and left a humid/sweltering prairie heat pulsing
against the walls and windows, he thought about how he could rid
himself of every emotional trauma he'd ever experienced. Why
hold onto them? he wondered. Why not eliminate them in sleep, in
waste, in breath? Why hold onto these things that keep us from
living?

Then, he slept with the thought of her returning to him
tomorrow. That thought stayed just behind his eyes with the image
of her waking him in the morning.

Next morning, he woke up when his nurse checked on him.
He kept his eyes closed, wanting her to just have Ashlee come
into his room, but then he opened his eyes on second thought. He
didn't want her to tell Ashlee he was sleeping.

"Do I have any visitors?"

"No, not that I know of."

"Are you sure?"

"I'll check for you."

"Great. Do you remember when my wife said she would be back today? I mean, did she give a time? I didn't want to expect her any minute if she said she'll be back at a certain time. Ya know what I mean?"

"She wasn't specific. I don't recall."

"Okay."

When she left his room, he sat up gingerly on his bandaged buns and turned on the TV with the remote, surfing news stations, but nothing from Hannibal or Jerome.

As Pell drove his rental car into Iowa City, he was listening intently to Ashlee, for the last few days had been hectic with both putting time and energy into a cause they believed in—Destroy Missouri Madness.

"If he can't come back with us, he can find his own way back. He's a big boy. We don't need him for this, do we?" she asked the actor as he turned onto a one-way street downtown, soon parking in front of a Bohemian coffee house.

Pell put on his baseball cap and sunglasses before getting out of his rental car with Ashlee.

"We have to talk. Let's walk," he said.

He lit one of his Canadian cigarettes as they walked along the broad sidewalk teaming with retail shops and summer students going to and from classes. He told her that he didn't think that she realized how important it was that he remain anonymous during this thing.

"No, I do," she said.

"I don't believe you do, Ashlee. You see: J. D. is the key to all of this. I was the one who sent word to him about your family's bank in Thorpe."

"Who told you?"

"I can't tell you that now. And that's not even important now. All you should know is that I had to have that deed in order to have a chance at making this work. Your work to protect your family is done. And you've done a splendid job. But that's only an image and not as important as my career or finishing the job we have to do. Is that clear?"

"Yes."

"Good," he smiled, then he went over to an ashtray near a bench and butted his cigarette.

"How about some coffee?" he smiled.

"Sure."

They headed back for the coffee house near his rental car. She thought about how she really was looking forward to seeing J. D. Pell caught her thinking about J. D.

"You love him, don't you?"

"Yes," she smiled.

Pell waited in the car as Ashlee walked into the hospital. Soon, she came out alone.

"He's gone," she told Pell.

"Gone?"

"He checked out. He wrote a check for his medical bill and left."

"How long ago?"

"Over an hour."

Pell sped away from the hospital and soon was driving fast on I-80 headed back to Missouri. As Ashlee kept looking for the highway patrol, she said to Pell:

"He wouldn't have taken a bus. Either a cab or a rental car."

"Does he have any credit cards?"

"I don't think so," she said. "Why wouldn't he wait for us? I left word I'd be back today."

"Maybe he heard about the casino. Maybe he called the paper and found out there was no obituary for Albert Linn. He knows you've got his money. He's confused and got the hell out of there."

"We have to find him before he blows everything," she stressed. "I should've called him."

J. D. got out of the cab after the driver opened the back

door for him.

"I'll be right back."

The cab driver watched his fare go into the Jerome Café after he lit a cigarette.

The café was crowded for dinner. He could smell the liver and onions special printed on the chalkboard when he walked up to the register. Most of the small-talk chatting stopped when he raised his bandaged hands to the counter. They were quiet so they could hear him say:

"Hi, I'm Jack Dunn. I eat in here all the time. I have a cab waiting outside. Can I write a check for cash to pay him?"

"How much?"

"A hundred and eighty, no, two hundred."

She checked her cash drawer. "Yeah, I guess," she said stiffly.

"Thanks. Could you get my checkbook out of my shirt pocket?"

He leaned his chest closer to her. She removed the checkbook from his pocket and then he asked her to please make the check out for two hundred dollars. After she filled out the check, the café customers listened and watched.

"Could you please put the pen in my mouth so I can sign it? Oh, and if you could hold the check in place on the counter for me so it doesn't get away."

The café was so quiet as J. D. signed the check with his mouth. She took the pen gingerly from his mouth then gave him his cash.

"Thanks for doin' that. Oh, did they have Albert's funeral yet?"

"Albert?"

"Albert Linn. He died of a heart attack four or five days ago."

She snorted out her reply. "Albert was in for lunch today."

"We are talkin' about Albert the town cop, right?" She nodded yes. He looked around at the puzzled faces who looked away from his gaze when his eyes hit theirs. For five or ten seconds, he stood there gape-jawed like a deer frozen in headlights. He flashed back to Pell driving Albert's patrol car and asking his cab driver for directions to the hospital.

He left the café in a fog with most of the patrons shaking their heads at Ray Dunn's grandson, the man who telemarketed from a treehouse; the man who sold Kedloe's land to Stone.

After he paid the Iowa City cab driver: "Come on, man, I'll give ya a ride to yer car."

"No, thanks, I gotta walk."

J.D. walked across the street as if walking in a fog of confusion. J. D. could see that he was walking down the same residential street in the dream he had while in surgery, where the scarred boy Hammon was on the bed being nursed by his mother during her plangent grief.

Now, up the hill, looking into the sun, he could see one of Stone's antique school buses coming toward him, the smooth shift from its automatic transmission was barely audible as it parked alongside the Old School grounds.

He could see the tour driver's mouth moving fast while she pointed to the ground where the row of bodies was covered with blankets. Just then, J. D. flashed back to old man Cochrand at the cupola telling Stone about finding his son under the last blanket. He then saw Cochrand's burning body in the burning rental car and Ashlee—showing him the statue of the little girl holding the kitten.

He walked down the street headed for Albert's house. He knew just where the house was even though he hadn't been there since he was a boy.

"Why?" he asked himself out loud.

Albert's house used to be George Hammon's house, the same house he saw in the dream. Linn was printed on the mailbox in front of the house. The patrol car was gone. Then he saw something inside Albert's garage that made him hurl onto the driveway—it was a yellow-handled chainsaw hanging on the wall. He saw the bold black printed letters WY printed on the motor of the chainsaw.

He hurried away from Albert's house, his hands beginning to throb for the first time since he left Iowa City. Stone's tourists were walking about and standing on the Old School grounds, some taking photographs with their cameras. The tour guide/driver was having a smoke while she pointed out the location of the school blast when Ray Dunn's grandson drove away with the Missouri Madness tour bus.

He floored the bus with no idea where he was headed. His improvised plan was to get Albert to come to him. And for some reason, when he came to that fork in the road to either go to Sunnyside or not, he chose Sunnyside, and soon found himself parking Stone's bus in front of the retirement home. He hurried inside without a clue why he was looking for Jerome survivors and completely oblivious to the staff.

They were all there, packed in the dining room, some on wheelchairs, quiet, some asleep where they sat. He went to the center of the room and yelled at the top of his lungs.

"SURVIVORS! LISTEN TO ME!"

The kitchen staff froze to listen to what the crazy man with the bandaged hands wanted. Again, but this time he roared from his belly and his sound was powerful without the strain:

"Survivors. I'm sorry I sold Kedloe's land. If you go with me now..I have a good shot at making things right. I can't do it alone. Will you help me?"

He surveyed the room. One by one a survivor stood up at his table or waved an arm. J. D. helped one elderly survivor to her feet. Just then, J. D. could see a nurse head for a phone. He ran over to her and held down the phone's flashhook with a bandaged hand and asked her to please give them five minutes before she called the police. She looked around the dining room at the plaintive faces of the survivors. She put the phone receiver down quietly.

"I'll wait five minutes..after you've left," she said.

"Thank you."

J. D. turned to the room of survivors. "Survivors, outside!"

He started to escort survivors out of the dining room with the kitchen staff now helping them leave.

Stone was roaming his casino floor among beefed-up

security. He was smiling at customers as if he had everything under his control and that all is well, when one of his staff hurried up to him, breathing hard. Stone looked hard at his employee as if this better not be bad news and he better keep his voice down.

"Mr. Stone, sir, your security guard in Jerome is on your line. He says it's an emergency." Stone left the room with a fake courtesy smile under his moustache.

Pell's speedometer was on ninety when he left Iowa and crossed the Missouri state line.

Stone took the call in his office. On the phone, his guard at Missouri Madness told him his bus had been stolen by that crazy guy across the road. He asked his boss if he should call Chief Linn. Stone looked at his watch.

"That was the last tour?" he asked his guard.

"Yes, sir."

"No, don't call anybody. Ya hear me?"

"Yes, sir."

"Make sure those tourists are picked up by another bus immediately. And get everyone out of there. That means you, too."

Stone slammed down his phone receiver, then he quickly found Albert's phone number to his patrol car on his rolodex. He called the number but there was no answer. He exited his office in a hurry.

Albert's patrol car was parked near Turtle Lake, where Linn took his daily walk maybe twice a week at the most. Albert's limp was more pronounced than usual as he walked with George Hammon. The scarred old man's hands are clasped behind his back as he listened to his friend.

"Just stay with the script, George. Remember what Pell told you. And don't worry about Stone. He won't know it's for real until it's too late to do anything about it."

"What if he tries to stop me?" George said.

"He won't."

They reached the patrol car. Albert opened the trunk. Several one-gallon cans of gasoline are inside the trunk with J. D.'s safe deposit box. Albert finished his point.

"Stone's getting two hundred thousand bucks for this rehearsal."

"Ray's grandson's money?" George asked.

"No, Ray's."

Albert opened the safe deposit box and took out the deed to Kedloe's land. "But this is all worth it, George. Every dime. Two devils will die today, George. Mark my word."

Sixteen survivors were wide-eyed, seated on Stone's bus. J. D. counted them, noting half men and half women. They were so quiet, like when they were children so long ago. These were the children of soft-spoken parents who taught them to suffer quietly, though they had been murdered in their most sacred of places—the Old School. This was the place where their parents learned to read and write and trust. They all trusted men like Kedloe to protect the children of the children.

Still, J. D. had no clue what he was doing with these people, and his time was running with the engine, for it was painful to turn the ignition with both bandaged hands squeezed together. His hands were on fire from starting the bus at the Old School grounds. He could feel the grafted skin's diaphanous cover throbbing palpably under the bandages. He closed the bus door and turned on the A/C before driving away, slowly at first; then, he picked up speed, not sure WY, but he knew where he was going.

He drove faster and faster, still not knowing or thinking about what would happen. This, he knew, was the ultimate time to let things happen and go with the flow. Planning ahead, what to do next, all seemed unnecessary now. This was something he had never done before consciously, and there were sixteen elderly children that trusted him now. His shoulders were not tense as usual, his feet and hands and other places were not perspiring; and if he could take his eyes off the road and his bandaged paws at the top of the wheel and look into the mirror, he would see the death of J. D., the King of Slugs, and see the true light of Ray Dunn's only grandson and executor.."So Alive."

When he hit the county road where just ahead Mr. Cochrand died, he saw what Cochrand saw: the little girl holding the kitten. But he plowed right through it without flinching, his course as steady as if Ray Dunn himself was escorting these special people to a place where their demon had slept, worked, and lived among them, all the while plotting the death and destruction of the most precious thing to any town on earth—its children.

And there they were, every single one of his sixteen passengers was here for the same reason he was here right now; not for what Kedloe did to them personally or their classmates and teachers. They were here for the pain Kedloe caused their parents. The bruises, blood, cuts and traumas would fade into scars; it was the grief in the eyes of their parents that put them on the bus with the man who made this all possible—resolution at last.

Up ahead he could see the ashes of Oz and his Grandpa Dunn's house. He had to brake now in order to turn onto the property across the road. He saw the empty guardshack and not a soul in sight. Some things were not right. People should be here now.

He parked behind the barn out of view from the front of the place. He turned off the engine and stood in the aisle at the front of the bus and faced his passengers.

"I'm going in. I can't tell you what to do, but I gotta do somethin'."

They watched him exit the bus and vanish around the corner of the barn.

When he approached the front of the Kedloe house, Pell drove in with Ashlee. He parked his rental near the house. He was wearing sunglasses and the same cap. J. D. did not trust anybody at this point. She got out of the car and went after J. D., anxious to explain.

"Why didn't you wait? We just got back from Iowa City."

She followed him onto the open front porch and persisted, warning him, "You can't be here now, J. D."

Just then, when J. D. saw Stone's Cadillac drive onto his property, he ducked inside the house with Ashlee in pursuit.

Inside the house, J. D. was looking around for something, he wasn't sure what, as Ashlee stayed with him, not wanting to tell him what was going down right now.

"J. D., we've got this thing going on now where Stone gets money because he thinks we're here with Pell to rehearse a movie, and..."

"How much money? Two hundred and fifty thousand, Ashlee? My money, Ashlee?"

"Two hundred thousand! And, yes! It's your money! And Ray's money! Mine! And everybody else in this town that doesn't want this!" She watched him looking in cupboards in the kitchen for something.

"What are you looking for?"

He didn't know. So, he said nothing, and went over to the front room picture window and looked through the part in the curtains at Stone and Pell standing near Stone's Cadillac. Stone was glad-handing the celebrity and his every word could be heard through the cheap materials used for the house. They both listened to Stone's words.

"Mr. Pell, I'm such a big fan of yours. You have no idea what a big fan I am of yours. I do hope you will consider giving me just a small, tiny little part, no lines, I don't need lines, but I could be an extra. But no big deal, Mr. Pell. Oh, by the way, do you have the money?"

"Mr. Linn is bringing it."

"Oh, good, I have a job for him too. Have you seen that crazy J. D.? He's got one of my buses."

J. D. looked over at the Kedloe mannequin sitting in the chair. He went over to it, he bent down, picked up the chair and mannequin and violently heaved it through the front room picture window. For a moment, Stone and Pell were both shocked to see the star of Missouri Madness face-down on the front porch with his favorite chair on top of him.

The actor was caught off guard by just how much he did resemble Kedloe, the likeness uncanny, he thought. Pell got an instant headache. He knew his body well and that meant stress was on the assault. J. D. exited the house with Ashlee on his heels just when Stone saw Albert driving toward them on the county road.

"You're going to jail, Dunn!" Stone blared.

A big smile came over Stone's face when he added: "Unless you are ready to sell me that land."

Stone's smile vanished when he saw George Hammon's face behind Albert's front passenger window. Stone realized if not for the law—he'd be trapped like a rat. The rat told Linn to arrest J. D. for this property damage and for stealing his bus.

Pell's shaded eyes were on Hammon's scarred face as the self-effacing survivor sat in the patrol car with his chin dipped into his chest, for quiet George was purposely avoiding the Kedloe mannequin.

Albert went to his trunk and opened it. That's when Albert broke the news to Stone.

"Ya know, Stone, when I gave your man my chainsaw, it was because I wanted J. D. out of town for sellin' you this ground. I just wanted him gone. Then, Mr. Pell here, had me read his script that was mailed to me from California. I read about the best way to make my problems go away without going away myself."

"What are you talking about, Linn! Arrest this man!" Stone demanded.

Albert removed his holstered handgun from his trunk and attached the holster to his belt so that his gun rode his hip. "Mr. Pell helped J. D. find this," he told Stone.

Albert waved the Kedloe property deed at Stone from J. D. 's safe deposit box.

"What is that?" Stone demanded.

"It's the original deed to Kedloe's property. And with all these witnesses, I don't need anything but your signature on it, Stone. No courthouse red tape, just your signature."

"I'm not signing anything! What is this?" Stone demanded. "Oh, I get it, this is part of the script, right?" Stone laughed.

Stone started to walk toward getting into his Cadillac when

Albert fired off a round from his gun into the mannequin's head which froze Stone in his tracks.

"George!" Albert called out.

When Hammon got out of the patrol car, Albert told the scarred old man to park Stone's car in the Kedloe barn. When Hammon drove toward the barn, Pell came over to Chief Linn and mumbled about how he didn't recall anything about putting Stone's car in the barn. Albert told Pell that he made a few revisions to the script as Albert limped over to the actor's rental car and removed the key from the ignition, leaving the trunk of his patrol car open. Pell could see all the gas cans in the trunk.

"I can't be a part of this," the actor said as he backed away toward the county road, wanting to leave the scene before something crazy happened.

Albert told Pell: "You're not going anywhere. Don't make me shoot the star."

Albert holstered his gun when Pell stepped back toward the group when Stone started some jibberish about how Albert is supposed to be the law.

That's when J. D. spoke up. "This isn't about the law, Stone."

"Albert, I'm with ya on this, but I think you should know that I've got sixteen people from Sunnyside..." J. D. said to Geronimo.

Just then, the survivors came walking toward them slowly from behind the barn, some were helping some to walk. Ashlee ran over to them as Albert tried to figure out what he was going to do with this group from Sunnyside. Pell turned his face away so the survivors could not see him.

"J. D., you are somethin' else. Why did you bring them here?" Albert asked J. D.

"I don't know."

"What am I s'posed to do with all those people, J. D.?"

"Albert, I just brought 'em here. I don't know..."

He froze on his next word: WY, the same word in his dream in the hospital. J. D. looked at Albert, then over to Pell as Stone's rat-like eyes moved back and forth.

"Everybody into the barn!" Linn barked.

J. D. turned to the survivors, all huddled around Ashlee, then he looked at Albert. Then, over to Pell. He knew Pell was the key to WY.

Albert's right hand cupped over his holster made Stone and Pell move along toward the barn. Hammon waited at the barn's open double door as if this was part of a plan. Hammon kept his head bowed submissively because of Ashlee—he had always been shy and self-conscious around attractive women.

Albert lit a kerosene lamp when Hammon closed them all in the barn with Hammon guarding the door from inside the barn. Albert addressed the group.

"We're buying back this property. " Albert removed the envelope holding J. D.'s cash that Ray left him in the safe deposit box. J. D. kept quiet as Pell slinked out of view in the shadows to avoid being identified.

"What are you talking about?" Stone demanded.

"I'm not just talkin', Stone. Here's your two hundred thousand back. You'll sign this deed over to me and you'll get your insurance money after we torch this place. Pretty simple, huh?"

"I'm not signing anything and you're not torching anything! Now, I'm getting out of here!"

Hammon blocked the door. Stone turned, looked at the group and started to walk toward his car at the other end of the barn. Albert pulled his gun and fired a round over Stone's head. Stone turned back to Albert.

"Oh, I get it, the script, never mind," he half-laughed his scared laugh.

Albert was losing his patience. J. D. was confused about a script and he wasn't sure what was going on here. Then Albert ordered Stone back over to his mark and told J. D. to get those people out of here. One survivor shouted "NO!", then another. And another. Albert continued to Stone:

"I don't want to shoot you. But what do you expect. I'm too old to strangle ya. Or beat your greedy little brains out. Stone, you're hurtin' good people for greed. Your problem is, this place is gone tonight and you with it because I can't figure out a way to keep you from sendin' us to jail. I can't trust ya to keep your mouth shut if I let ya slide outta here on your belly..you friggin' snake."

All eyes were on Stone as he pleaded for his life because he could see that he had no allies here.

"You want a percentage of the take? Huh? You got it! Whatever you want! I'm easy! We can make a deal here!"

Albert removed his gun from his holster and offered it to Hammon. "George, you wanna do this?"

When Hammon went over to Albert to take his gun, Pell said anxiously, "Stay with the script, Linn."

"I'll sign the deed, anything!" Stone begged. Albert dropped his gun to his thigh and Ashlee went over to Albert and got the deed and a pen from Linn. Ashlee took the deed over to Stone and had Stone sign it on the right spot.

"Make sure he dates it," J. D. reminded Ashlee.

Albert went over to Stone and gave him the envelope that held J. D.'s two hundred thousand dollars. Just then, one of the scarred survivors yelled out from the huddled mass of survivors in the dimly-lit barn. "You can't trust him!"

Stone looked around the barn at all the characters and burst out into laughter.

"I'm sorry..but that deed looked like the real thing and these people were not in the script and I lost my focus when one of them yelled at me," he explained.

"Just stay with the script," Pell repeated.

Albert rolled his eyes at Ashlee when Stone pointed to his car and asked if he could get his script and said while he headed for his passenger side of his car: "Okay, this is where I get my gun out of the glovebox."

When Stone got his handgun out of his glovebox, he was confused how his gun got there. He checked it quickly to make sure it was not loaded. When he came back over to his mark, he said to Albert:

"This is my gun. I didn't bring it. I keep it in my desk drawer in my office. How did it get in my glovebox?"

J. D. could see what was happening as Albert warned J. D. that he better get those people out of here.

"Stay with the script, Linn," Pell repeated as Albert aimed his gun at Stone.

J. D. intervened with bandaged hands throbbing. "I did this, Albert! I made this happen! If it wasn't Stone, it would've been someone else! I sold out for the money!"

As Stone cowered when Albert was about to pull the trigger, J. D. stepped in front of Stone in Albert's line of fire. Albert told Ashlee to get the survivors out of the barn.

"NO!" J. D. shouted. "You want us to get away with murder like Kedloe did!"

He pointed at Pell. "Tell them who you are and why you're here!"

J. D. went over to Hammon and took the lantern from the scarred survivor, holding the lantern painfully between both bandaged hands. He then went over to Pell and raised the light to Pell's face.

"Take off that cap and glasses!" J. D. demanded. "You can't come here disguised with your clever Hollywood script, have us play a part in murdering this man and expect us not to ask why! Why are you here?"

Pell removed his cap and glasses. Some of the survivors including Hammon were shocked to see just how much the stranger resembled the man who tried to murder them. Pell kept his eyes low on the barn floor as if ashamed. He could hear some of the survivors move closer to him to get a better look at him, and then gasp when they saw the resemblance to Kedloe, the monster who murdered their village so many years ago. J. D. could see Pell resisting the urge to tell them anything. Then, J. D. whispered to the actor. "Why? Why are you here?"

Pell thought about going for Albert's gun and blowing Stone's brains out as the script read. His voice was soft and emotional as he faced his audience that listened so intently.

"My father was Kedloe's half-brother. He was living in Tecumseh in 1927. He disowned the name, changed his name and had nothing to do with any of them. He moved to London two months after the disaster. I found this out after I acquired fame as an actor when I researched my family tree. My father never spoke of his past, his life in America. A not-so-good friend wrote a script about this when I told him about my connection to it. When he found out about Stone's plans to build this place, he blackmailed me into buying the rights to it or he'd sell it to a studio. I wanted to make sure nobody found out I was related to that monster."

"I've got witnesses here that you torched this place for the insurance money if you ever open your mouth about what happened here tonight," Albert told Stone. "Be happy you got your money back you paid J. D. for this land and the money you'll get from the insurance company for what you put into this place. And, you got your life back. Is that fair, Stone?"

Stone thought that was more than fair, nodding yes.

"George! Do what Mr. Cochrand wanted to do," Albert said.

Hammon exited the barn. Albert limped over to Stone and snatched the script out of his hands. "I'll shoot your brains out if you call the fire department or press charges or say anything about what happened here tonight. You know I will, don't ya, Stone."

Stone nodded yes, then Albert told him to beat it before he changed his mind.

After Stone drove his Cadillac out of the barn, J. D. asked Albert where Stone's security guard was.

"I told him Pell said no witnesses or no dough."

Hammon, Pell, Ashlee and J. D. and most of the survivors took part in pouring gas inside the house and barn from the gasoline containers in Albert's trunk.

They were all grouped outside when Chief Linn handed George Hammon a lit torch made from tightly wound newspapers soaked in gasoline. They all watched the most scarred survivor put the torch to the Kedloe mannequin outside near the front room window. They cheered when Hammon tossed the burning Kedloe likeness and chair through the window, whereupon flames began to spread fast inside the house. Next, Hammon torched the barn and guardshack.

A little later, seventeen survivors, including George Hammon, are all teary-eyed as they watch the Kedloe house and barn burn out of control. They all held hands, forming a human barricade that blocked the only entrance onto Missouri Madness. Albert called the Jerome Volunteer Fire Department a few minutes earlier. The approaching siren could be heard from Geronimo's parked patrol car behind the ashes of Oz and Ray Dunn's house. J. D. and Ashlee sat in the back of the patrol car with Albert behind the wheel as they stared straight ahead, watching the flames across the road.

"Why'd you torch my tree?" J. D. asked Albert.

"I told Stone it would get you to sell him Ray's land."

"And so Stone trusted you after that," Ashlee added, then, Albert nodded in agreement while he kept his focus on the flames.

Albert stayed in his car for as long as he could, watching the flashing red firetruck stalled at the entrance to the Kedloe land as firemen tried in vain to get the elderly survivors to move away from the entrance. They watched firemen plead with the survivors, but they could not be sundered or persuaded to budge an inch.

When the cheaply-made Kedloe house and barn were crumbling into cinder and ash, Albert turned on his blue flashers and drove forward to the Dunn entrance and parked there with his flashers on. Chief Linn took his time going over to the survivors and helpless firemen as Ashlee and J. D. stayed in the back seat, holding hands while watching the end of Missouri Madness.

Later that winter, in the early afternoon, he was seated on a purple beach towel. J. D. dug his lily-white toes into the hot white Bahama sand and began to play "So Alive" by Love and Rockets on his portable CD player.

Quickly, he put on his sunglasses. He wanted to see her coming; he knew she would, for his dream girl was no longer a dream. As the song played, he looked down to his hands that were now completely healed and as flexible as ever. He looked down the beach. He couldn't see her yet. Could she hear the music? he wondered.

For a few moments, he forgot about her and was lost in the music, the heat, the sand, the blue water and horizon, but mostly the music had brought it back for him—in waves of golden feathers that tickled him now right on his heart. He sold his grandfather's land to George Hammon for one dollar, and the disaster's most scarred survivor was now registered in the Hannibal Courthouse as owner of the Kedloe property. Stone got paid by his insurance company and never pressed charges. Albert retired in October. Albert's retirement party was held in Ashlee's house in Thorpe. Over three hundred people showed. George Hammon and J. D. went for a walk alone. They strolled past the Thorpe bank that Ashlee's family owned. George talked about how his life shut down after he was injured in the disaster, and how Ray Dunn was the only person who helped him get through that. That's when J. D. asked George if he was looking for the deed to Kedloe's land in his grandpa's coffin in the funeral home.

"Oh, no!" George laughed. "I had put a note inside his jacket pocket next to his heart."

"I'm curious what the note said," J. D. smiled.

George explained, his voice broke with emotion at times. "The next school year, I was afraid to go back to school. I had nightmares about it. I really dreaded going back there. I didn't talk much at all after the school blew up. I would write out my answers on notes, usually with a yes or no. Ray came over to my house, said he wanted me to go back to school so I could learn how to read and write. I wrote on a note: WY, not knowing how to spell why. He laughed and corrected me. That's what I put in the note: "WY".

J. D. didn't tell George about his dream in the hospital with the WY; instead, he kept quiet and thought about the mood he was in just after he caught George in the funeral home that day, and how his perceptions and feelings about the disaster had certainly played out in his moods when awake and in his dreams. Would things have been different if this quiet man who was so badly scarred by a monster had explained to him there and then in the funeral home about the WY he was placing in Grandpa Ray's pocket?

On his beach towel, he smiled to himself as "So Alive" played from his CD player that stood on the Bahama sand. Just then, he looked down the stretch of white sand where the foamline from passive waves enveloped her brown ankles. Her thong bikini was passion red against her brown skin. When she moved closer, she smiled long at him, as if she loved him. Quickly, he changed CDs and turned up the volume before he caught up to her running on the wet sand just after the end of a new wave. They could hear Merle Haggard's "That's the Way Love Goes" playing above the gentle surf.

She smiled at him as they walked along the sand. She took his hand that he offered her. Her palm pressed onto his, right on the very same spot where his Grandpa Ray's safe deposit box key was branded into his flesh. She knew that; she massaged the smooth scar tissue in tiny circles with her fingertips. Then he stopped her and turned her to him, putting his arms around her. They began to slow-dance to the music like that night in her parents' kitchen, the night he missed his bubble bath and his chance to really see love again in the eyes of a woman who loved him.

THE END

Author's note: On May 18th, 1927, a madman devastated and emotionally destroyed a small town in America's Heartland. I first heard about this true disaster in 1980 and thought it the most incredible event I'd ever heard of—and still do.

Twice I went to this place to research this disaster and to write an original screenplay about it. I was encouraged by the most scarred survivor, he being the first to read my script when finished. But each time I left that town, I went away baffled, confused, and angry at the man responsible for so much suffering. I've communicated with dozens of survivors, mostly by letters exchanged and many second hand conversations with relatives and friends of survivors.

I soon realized I could not submit my finished script or any of the subsequent versions of the disaster I'd written over these last twenty years. Certain things became clear: I couldn't write about the actual place where this happened and possibly draw unwanted negative attention to the community; I couldn't attempt to write about the actual suffering of the victims or pretend to know what that was like for them; and I could not ever use the actual name of the monster who caused so much suffering, for I felt in some way this would glorify him in the annuls of darkness.

I wanted to create a contemporary story and get some sense of fictional justice out of it for the survivors, and yet show what man is capable of doing to man without all the gratuitous violence the medias feed us daily.

When something as tragic as this happens in a public school—it affects all of us no matter when it happened. When I was walking on the Old School grounds, I was told by a not-so-friendly survivor: "A writer ought to find better things to write about."

I thought about that a long time, and I discovered one thing about myself—I write to forget, to get it all out of me and move the thing along until satisfied that I might have helped someone, somewhere, somehow by doing so—even if that someone is me.

I am most happy to be into my next project now after

"Missouri Madness." God willing, this will be a series of novellas titled "Writer/In" with the first story of the series titled "Shy Ann." I hope you will want to read it. Many thanks to my libraries and readers who support me and keep me writing. Thanks again. Feedback always appreciated from my readers.

Michael Frederick
P. O. Box 8606
Asheville, NC 28814
(888) 810-1952